DON'T MESS WITH TESS!

Praise for the Tess Camillo series by Morgan Hunt

"Morgan Hunt continues to delight with this new offering [*Fool on the Hill*]. . . . This one is the whole package—characters who continue to grow, a great story, wonderful writing, and wicked humor."
—*OutSmart Magazine* (Houston)

"Author Morgan Hunt does it again with another excellent Tess Camillo mystery. . . . The story is fast paced and packed full of grisly murder, intrigue and humor."
—Cherie Fisher, *Reader Views*

"*Sticky Fingers* . . . is fast-moving and clever, raunchy and sexy, serious and funny; a delight to read."
—Marianne Moskowitz, *WomanSource Rising*

" . . . an engaging tale of equal parts murder, sharp dialogue, loss, and humor."
—Chelsea Fine, *Just Out*

"You will be fooled, which is half the fun of reading a mystery. Morgan Hunt gets better and better as a writer. Three cheers."
—Rita Mae Brown, *New York Times* best-selling author

"From beginning to end, *Fool on the Hill* is a thrill ride full of Camillo wit, spine-tingling fun and one terrific escape from reality, Morgan Hunt-style."
—LaRita M. Heet, Editor-in-Chief, *Jane and Jane Magazine*

"This is a terrific amateur sleuth tale . . . "
—*The Mystery Gazette*

"Glib, funny, heart-warming, and heartbreaking, Hunt pulls the strings and has . . . (the) reader thoroughly absorbed in Tess' life and antics before we can say 'snake-bite.' . . . Funny, colorful, quirky, and an absolute delight to read!"
—Alex Wolfe, *Kissed by Venus*

"Tess narrates with verve . . . an engaging swift read."
—Ethan Boatner, *Lavender Magazine*

"It's a genuine pleasure to read a mystery with smart writing. Morgan Hunt immediately captured my attention and made me shiver until learning the startling truth. I can't wait to read her next book."
—J. Miyoko Hensley, writer, *Murder, She Wrote*

"*Sticky Fingers* is a terrific amateur sleuth tale. . . . Readers will adore this middle-aged 'Criminitlies' woman whose noble significant other of the moment is her Welsh terrier, Raj."
—Harriet Klausner, *The Midwest Book Review*

BLINDED BY THE LIGHT

A TESS CAMILLO MYSTERY

MORGAN HUNT

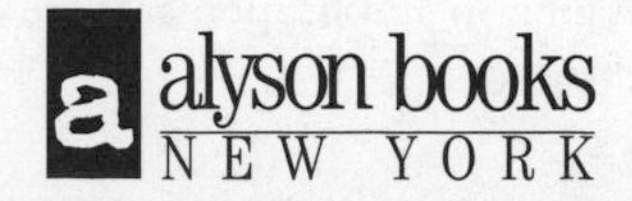

This story is fiction. The characters and events are products of the author's imagination. Any resemblance to actual events or persons, living or dead, is coincidental.

Manufactured in the United States of America

A trade paperback original published by Alyson Books
245 West 17th Street, New York, NY 10011

Distribution in the United Kingdom by Turnaround Publisher Services Ltd.
Unit 3, Olympia Trading Estate, Coburg Road, Wood Green
London N22 6TZ England

First Edition: August 2008

08 09 10 11 12 13 14 15 16 17 a 10 9 8 7 6 5 4 3 2 1

ISBN-10: 159350-085-8
ISBN-13: 978-1-59350-085-6

Library of Congress Cataloging-in-Publication data are on file.
Cover design by Victor Mingovits

For Karen

ACKNOWLEDGMENTS

This book is truly a community effort and I'd like to thank all who have contributed to it. In particular I'm grateful for the help of Philip R. Croft, MD, Office of the Medical Investigator, Albuquerque, NM; Juanita de la O Gordon, Chief Investigator, Office of the District Attorney, Seventh Judicial District, Socorro, NM; editor Sarah Van Arsdale; Eric Salberta; Lucy Warren, Master Gardener in San Diego; Mary Steward; Wendy Martin, MD; Anna Pulley; Deborah Hardesty, RN, BSN, LT USN ret.; Melissa Romero, City of Albuquerque Emergency Services; my Alpha Readers (Fran Brass, M. J. Daspit, and Karen Fitch); Assistant Professor Mary Carrabba and Associate Professor Greg Miller of Southern Oregon University; Devorah Zaslow; Shawn Phillips, for permission to use the lyrics of his song "The Ballad of Casey Deiss"; and Robin L. Hotchkiss, who co-wrote the Lana chapter.

1

NO HANDBASKET REQUIRED

BRISTLY BLACK LEGS OF foot-long tarantulas crawling over your naked body. In a locked room. Forever. That was the personal vision of hell of my best friend in high school. The unrelenting boredom of absolutely no sensory stimuli throughout eternity might be someone else's Hades. My own version of hell would include Ron Jeremy, long hypodermic needles, and a looping soundtrack of the Oz munchkins. I'll spare you further details.

As I raised my living room blinds on this mid-June morning, I knew that whatever Club Med of Misery lay beyond, it had a reservation with my name on it. What else could await someone who spent her morning nibbling apple butter on whole wheat, sipping Kona blend, and hoping for a murder?

Soft drizzle dappled the picture window. June is one of the few months when San Diego gets variation in weather, usually in the form of a heavy fog we call "June gloom." This morning the weather was like an ADD woman at a shoe store. It tried on this; it tried on that; fog mists here; sunshine and sprinkles there. Nothing seemed to please for more than a moment. Suddenly, an angled shaft of sunlight lanced through the room.

Since my thoughts were already on hell, I was reminded of Lucifer—the Morning Star, the bearer of light. I'd probably get to know him personally after wishing for murder. I didn't really want anyone specific to be killed, certainly not anyone I cared for. But in the real world, the Big Bad Wolf prowls. People do get murdered. And if it was going to happen anyway, I wanted to be tangential to the act, involved somehow in bringing to justice those who took human life. Synchronicity had enmeshed me in two murders already, and I was jonesing for the next adrenaline rush. My thrill thirst may have had something to do with the fact that my romantic and professional lives weren't exactly hot skittles at the moment.

As I stood there, a magnificent rainbow shimmered across my living room floor, and danced along the Guatemalan rug. If a rainbow could dance, so could I! In fact, I could tango. I put the *Frida* soundtrack in the stereo and turned up the volume.

My housemate, Lana Maki, and I enjoy dancing together. Back before Jesus spoke to a president about the righteousness of invading sovereign nations, back when W 43 was just the coked-up scion of an ex-CIA director, we'd danced a different dance together—the Great Dance that inspires all others. Lana was fey, Finnish, and feminine. And I fell. Hard. After dabbling in the lifestyle for a few years, Lana met a poet-boxer at her credit union one day, and soon made a withdrawal from my bed to his. Their relationship proved more haiku than epic, but it ended our affair. Since then we've lived together as housemates, moving through our lives with comfortable complementarity and a half-smile of things remembered.

The tango partner in my mind was Lana. The tango partner in my arms was an oversized bed pillow that never missed a beat. Step, glide, stomp! I snapped my head around to the beat. My pulse pranced and strutted along with the music—a *giro* here; a *barrida* there. All I needed was a rose between my teeth.

The rhythmic stomp of my feet was enough to dissuade my Welsh terrier, Raj, and Lana's "intellectually undistinguished" (that's the kindest way I can put it) dachshund, Pookie, from getting underfoot. Both dogs lurked in the kitchen, where they studied their food bowls as though the last few nibs of Science Diet were canine koans.

My fantasy dance was abridged by the ringing of the phone. When I noted the caller ID, I almost didn't pick up, but guilt poked me like one of Salma Hayek's high heels. It was my brother, Barry "the Baron" Camillo, calling from New Jersey. The Baron had taken his family to Africa for a month; it would be rude not to welcome him home.

As I picked up the receiver, I groped the end table for pen and paper. The Baron has the habit of going into infinite detail on every little thing in his universe, and when your brain has turned to pudding from boredom, he'll shrewdly question you about what he just said. I'd learned to make notes.

"Oh, the smells! The rain—it's just so different, Tess; you *have* to go. You and, you know, one of those chicks you hang with—whichever one is the flavor of the month—*go*. Start with Tanzania like we did. On the first safari, we saw eight black rhinos—imagine! Eight! There're, like, maybe ten in the whole world. And . . ."

I sank into the creamy leather of my living room sofa. My "Uh huh" met his "and water buffalo—nasty suckers!" My "wow" balanced his boast about how quickly he'd picked up pertinent Swahili phrases.

" . . . and Brooke even got to fly one of those paraglider things. We slipped one of the park rangers some American green, and next thing you know, there was my daughter—sailing over the African plains. 'Course, Bridget was so jealous she couldn't stand it, and turned into a total snot for the next three days."

As I stared at the living room fireplace, he came up for breath for a few seconds. I wondered if he'd asked me anything—anything—about my life. Ah, but there's a reason we nicknamed him the Baron.

He continued with fervor, "In Nairobi, we stayed in the Giraffe Manor. You actually feed giraffes from your hotel window! They stick their heads right in! I swear, Sis, this trip was . . . well, you're just going to have to see for yourself."

I jotted on the note pad: giraffes at hotel—fed through window? I wondered if I got that one right, and decided to pay closer attention. Another call came in; I put the Baron on hold and told my old friend Beth that I'd call her back. My brother picked up where he'd left off. I soon had a page and a half of notes covering everything from the quality of cassava in the Lilongwe market, to what he'd learned from a Kenyan bartender about Mau Mau oaths.

As the Baron started to wind down, he suddenly remembered who he was talking to. "How're you feeling these days?"

My brother was aware, as were all of my friends and family, that I'd had a recent mastectomy and breast reconstruction, thanks to a very aggressive carcinoma, not to mention a close encounter with a murderer only months ago.

"A few scars here and there, Baron, but I'm almost back to normal."

"You always were the strong one, Tess. And really, you *gotta* do this African trip. It's a once-in-a-lifetime opportunity."

He rang off before I had the chance to tell him what cancer had taught me: everything is a once-in-a-lifetime opportunity, even the chance to tango with a pillow.

2

BIRD'S-EYE VIEW

IF GOVERNMENT SPIES USED seagulls for surveillance (are you sure they don't?), they'd observe two La Jolla teens steering shiny Segways along Mission Beach boardwalk, stopping at a weather-beaten surf shop for a drug connection. They'd see a young Chicano adding a burst of turquoise to an outdoor mural in National City. If the seagulls swooped at just the right moment, they'd notice that the new manatee at SeaWorld likes to chase his own fart bubbles. Later, as smog and dampness press down on the long summer evening, those same avian spies might watch my solid size-16 butt sliding into the driver's seat of my silver FX.

I'd been feeling betwixt and between, like Michael Moore without a cause, for a few weeks now. My employer, the software giant Imitech, had eliminated my job, along with many others, in a re-org designed to leave stockholders ecstatic and employees bent forward, grasping their ankles—business as usual in corporate America. But after cancer and two close encounters with murder, a job layoff hardly registered on my personal Richter scale. I had current database and web programming skills and a degree in math. When I returned my friend's phone call yesterday, a new paycheck possibility had emerged, so I wasn't too concerned about work.

What did sap my serotonin were Lana's future plans. As Lana and I had set about solving one of San Diego's most gruesome murders last spring, we'd both met people we were attracted to. Lana's new fellow, a Feng Shui marketing exec, seemed like Mr. True Mensch. Maybe Mr. Right. The woman I'd met, an assistant music producer in L.A. named Nova, had had the good sense to cut and run when she realized my lifestyle frequently ran at Orange Alert.

I felt the satisfying engagement of the FX's gearshift as I backed out of my driveway. My humble home, with its chamois-colored stucco, birds of paradise, and purple passionflower vines, filled me with poignancy. A VA mortgage from my Navy service had made the house purchase possible, but even when I had a paycheck coming in, having a roommate was essential to keep the mortgage paid. It looked like Lana was on the fast-track for marriage. Who else could I live with that would be so compatible? Lana and I had learned each other's habits, preferences, and hot buttons. Breaking in a new housemate would take time, and unlike employment, there were no prospects on the horizon. Besides, losing Lana would be more than losing a housemate, and I wasn't ready to head in that direction just yet.

Instead, I headed through the streets of my comfortable Mission Hills neighborhood. Breezes blew through screen doors and sprinklers spurted. Pigeons scattered in the queen palms. Dogs welcomed people home. Cats celebrated yet another personal Independence Day and eyed the pigeons. At University Avenue, I turned east into Hillcrest; caught every possible red light in the gnarly traffic; and at Sixth, headed north onto 163. With the help of my 4-wheeled Silver Bullet, I zipped in and out of lanes, passing tentative tourists, and avoiding low riders who were high. San Diego traffic was beginning to rival L.A.'s, but the nimble Silver Bullet was up to the challenge. My left breast may have exited, stage right; my employer may have ditched my databases; my housemate might soon mate in another house; but damn it, my car could still cruise. At least that was something.

I took the 805 North exit, stayed in the far right lane, and followed the ramp east onto Balboa. I was meeting my friend Kari for burgers and a few games of pool at the Boll Weevil. The Weevil makes some of the best burgers in the city, and they serve them to you before they're cooked dry. In more ways than one, my life philosophy compels me to risk the rare *E. coli* if it means tasting the juice.

I'd just pulled into the Weevil's parking lot off Convoy when Kari's RAV4 entered from the opposite direction. I walked over to greet her, noticing the colorful bumper sticker: "My child is a shining star ☆ at Sandburg Elementary."

Kari's yellow jersey top and white Capri pants showed off her tawny skin and taut figure. Instead of her usual dreadlocks, she wore buttercup and hot pink scrunchies in her unbraided hair. She looked pretty good for a woman who packed more responsibility and stress into her life than anyone has a right to. As a hate crimes sergeant with the San Diego police, and the single mother of two, Kari certainly deserved whatever release a burger and a game of pool could provide.

I gave her a hug and gestured to the bumper sticker. "Looks like either Simone or Hunter inherited mom's brains."

"Definitely Simone. The day Hunter brings home a good report card is the day our city government will shine." In our city "mayoral election" is often a punch line. I laughed out loud, and we headed inside.

Our eyes soon adjusted to the dim interior of the Weevil, with its dark slat ceiling and rusty-farm-implement decor. The yeasty odor of a thousand beers smothered those of cow burger. A waitress right out of Mel's Diner led us to a table near the jukebox, and slid two menus in front of us. "Can I get you ladies something to drink?"

"Corona with lime," I replied, and Kari seconded the notion. We got down to the serious business of choosing between temptations like A-One-Derful Burger, The Big Daddy, and Honey-Stung Fried Chicken.

Forty-five minutes later, my cholesterol was higher, the air smelled yeastier, Jewel crooned from the jukebox, and I sank two stripes on the break. When I missed my next shot, Kari sank her orange, blue, and purple solids with downright elegance. She left me with an awkward shot: 10-ball in the corner pocket, with the 8-ball barely kissing it on the left. I leaned into the shot and tried to use about a quarter-tip of low left English. The shot went astray.

"These sticks are warped," I complained, as I finally exhaled. I enjoy shooting pool—its geometric lines and angles appeal to me—but my game was off this evening; I had a lot on my mind. I soon lost to Kari, and broke for stripes in our second game.

As I plotted a shot I knew I couldn't make, Kari sucked on the lime from her empty Corona. "Heard from Lana?"

"Got a postcard Tuesday. She and Gable are still at that lavender farm in Provençe, kicking back with some ex-pat friends of his." I signaled the waitress for two more brews. "Lana's Finnish, you know?" Kari nodded with minimal interest. "Somehow she managed to hook up with three Finnish tourists, out there in the French countryside. She and Gable invited them to dinner. I hope she doesn't come back with any experimental Finnish recipes."

The waitress delivered our Coronas. I tried a soft stroke with a bit of draw to execute a 12-15 combo, and keep the cue ball nearby. My shot worked; I'm good at soft stroking. "She and Gable were due back next Monday, but they extended their stay another week."

"Don't blame them. Sounds romantic." On her turn, Kari scratched. "While we're on romantic . . . Girl, how 'bout coming to my place tonight?"

Years ago, Kari and I had dated, but it hadn't worked. After that we'd traveled in different circles until fate drew me into two murder investigations, and her role as a police sergeant rekindled our friendship. With Lana in Europe and with no lover in my life, I'd taken to hanging out with Kari—a casual movie here, a few dances there. I should have known better; it was becoming obvious that she hoped for more than I could offer. Time to slow-roll the 9-ball in the corner pocket; time to break the news.

My shot rolled true. On the jukebox, Wynonna Judd lamented a broken heart.

"I appreciate the offer," I began, "but I've got a big trip ahead of me tomorrow. I'm leaving town for a while." I sank the 11 ball and went two rails for tight position on the 14.

Kari put her cue stick on the ground and stood up straight. "You're *leavin' town*? What for?"

I pocketed the 14, then got overconfident and scratched. "Remember my friend Beth Butler? Back in '99, she left UCSD's Supercomputer Department to become CIO of a software firm in Albuquerque. You must've heard me mention her." Kari, spotting the cue ball, merely nodded. "Well, Beth called me yesterday and offered me temp contract work there."

Kari sank her last solid, set herself up perfectly for the 8-ball, and won the game.

"I see my impending departure hasn't hurt your pool skills."

She tucked her cue stick into its holder along the wall and brushed blue chalk dust from the front of her yellow blouse. "Girl, you can be a real . . ."

A hefty guy bumped into her on his way to the men's room, managing to turn the not-so-accidental contact into something salacious. Kari, who had once been in an abusive marriage, has a very short fuse for that shit.

"B . . . ," he began, but she had the guy in a choke hold before he could "itch."

She flashed her badge. "I don't appreciate you coppin' a feel when you walk by." Our fellow Weevil customers looked anxious. Kari released her hold. "Get near us again and I'll book you for attempted assault."

He was soon gone with the whiz.

The interaction apparently helped dissipate any tension between us. We sipped our last Corona, and chatted about her kids. Eventually she asked, "So what kind of work has Beth got for you?"

"Her outfit nailed a government contract to data mine pharmacies for purchases of cold and flu medicines."

"To see who's buying meth-lab ingredients?"

"No, more like an early warning system for possible bioterror attacks. It's based on pattern recognition algorithms." Kari's expression told me the concept was still fuzzy. "If lots of people in an area suddenly experience flu-like symptoms, it *might* indicate a bioterrorist strike."

"Or ptomaine at the local salad bars." With the hand that used to hold cigarettes when she was a smoker, Kari twisted the scrunchies in her hair.

"That's where my work comes in. I'll be refining a program that recognizes normal flu medicine purchase patterns. The software will be able to tell when a pattern is out of the ordinary."

Kari smiled. "I can't believe you, of all people, will be working for Homeland Security."

"Hey, I was once married to a guy who works for a top spook agency." I picked up a leftover French fry. "Besides, Beth's contract isn't with Homeland Security."

"Who else tries to detect bioterrorism?"

"Anti-terrorism's big business, Kari; every government contractor is after a piece of the pie. The government's got more creepy divisions and departments snooping and experimenting and researching, seducing our tax dollars and eroding our rights, than the average schmoe would believe possible. And unfortunately, as the daily news graphically demonstrates, we're still not really 'secure'."

"I thought the Feds got organized after 9/11; doesn't the Department of Homeland Security coordinate everything now?"

"Neither the FBI, NSA, nor the CIA is under Homeland Security. They all report to the Director of National Intelligence, in parallel with Homeland Security. The Department of Defense has been especially creative—almost all of their spook functions are hidden from both Homeland Security *and* DNI overview. You don't hear about DARPA or DIA or DSS much, do you? Or my favorite, the Defense Security Cooperation Agency? 'Cooperation'—what a joke! Federal turf battles are just like the ones you complain about at SDPD, only more expensive."

"But doesn't that mean a lot of duplicated effort and cost inefficiencies?"

"Give this woman a cigar! Believe me, the official right hand of Homeland Security doesn't know what the unofficial left hand is doing."

Kari shook her head in disbelief. We headed for the parking lot. "How long you gonna be gone?"

"Beth said the work should last a few weeks. They've already done the basics."

"Got someone to take care of the dogs until Lana gets back?"

"Remember my neighbor Smacker?"

"Good-lookin' kid about twenty; sings rap, right?"

I nodded. "He'll take care of Raj and Pookie."

Kari unlocked the door of her RAV4 and turned to me. "Gonna miss you." The voice of this tough police sergeant sounded as shaky as Larry "wide stance" Craig's political future.

I hugged her long and tight. She felt good in my arms; smelled good, too. I began to reconsider her overnight invitation, but some high school punks at a nearby taco stand started yelling cat calls, which interrupted the mood. I suppose the sight of two women being that close for that long exceeded their hormonal tolerance levels. We broke the embrace. "I'll call when I get back in town."

"Keep your ass out of trouble, OK? I'm not gonna be there in New Mexico to help you out."

I waved good-bye and watched as her RAV4 bumped through the parking lot potholes and out onto the street.

Back home, I packed for the trip. I pressed my weight against one big suitcase to latch it. The suitcase was on my bed; leaning on it brought me closer to the side where no one sleeps; closer to the pillow I'd tangoed with. On a whim and a whoosh of loneliness, I decided to place an online personal ad. I booted up; navigated to PlanetOut; uploaded a recent photo; and wrote:

> If you enjoy tearing the wings off butterflies; if you're only in the mood when your moon's in Pluto; or if you only communicate by satellite, move to the next ad. I'm an attractive GWF, late 40s, brown/brown, 5′5″, size 16. I look a little like Isabella Rossellini, at least after I've had my coffee. Seeking educated, emotionally stable woman with sense of humor who's open to conversation, imagination, and osculation. (Look it up). Let's sit barefoot on my back patio, gaze at the stars, and tear the foil off a bottle of champagne.

I added information about my favorite movies, books, and activities, then saved the ad, shut down the computer, and got ready for bed. Big day ahead of me tomorrow; little dogs beside me tonight.

3

CRAZED WEASELS

THE SUMMER EVENING STILL held plenty of light, even after I'd settled into the efficiency suite I would call home for the next few weeks. I opened a window, seeking a breeze, but the air was still. Weird Al Yankovich once wrote a song in which he claimed that Albuquerque air smells like warm root beer. I suspected the scent drifting my way was more likely a combination of sun-baked sagebrush, *ristras* of dried chilies, and the neoprene of hot air balloons. In the same song, Weird Al also claimed that Albuquerque donut vendors sell boxes of crazed weasels, a myth I preferred not to explore during my work assignment.

I spent the next morning, my first on the job, at the offices of Bryce Corporation slogging through the obligatory mire of orientation paperwork. By early afternoon, my eyes were crossing, and I was relieved to see Beth come into the HR conference room.

"Come with me!" she whispered.

I grabbed my fanny pack and tailed Beth out of the building. Her robust body seemed a tad stockier. She'd added blond highlights to her golden brown hair; her jade eyes and clear complexion looked radiant. Apparently life in the city of donut weasels agreed with her.

"Where're we going?" I inquired as we approached the University of New Mexico campus. Beth steered her Accord off Central Avenue and onto Cornell, where a row of one-story commercial buildings lined the street.

"If you want the best barbecue in the southwest, you go to El Paso. You want the best New England clam chowder, you go to Boston . . . "

"And for the best fish tacos, I'll go to Baja, but where're we headed right now?"

Beth pulled into a parking place and turned off the ignition. "I had a craving for pizza. If you want the best pizza in Albuquerque, you go to Saggio's," she answered. "I'd say 'their crust is to die for,' but lately you have an uncanny knack for attracting corpses. Follow me."

The heat slapped me as we left the air-conditioned car and backtracked half a block. Saggio's was quite spacious inside. A long line of customers led to an order counter. Colors splattered the interior, as if several kaleidoscopes had recently lost their virginity here. A bright yellow vintage Mercedes displayed bakery items from under its hood. Roman columns topped with potted palms interspersed the tables and mauve-upholstered booths. Vines climbed and crept everywhere. Workers bustled about. I studied the menus posted overhead. Pastas, salads, and calzones beckoned, but Beth strongly urged pizza. I was happy to take her advice. Near the cash register grew a spiky Brobdingnagian bromeliad, reminiscent of the Little Shop of Horrors. I tendered my cash with care.

"Different atmosphere, isn't it?" Beth asked, gesturing around.

"Mediterranean on mescaline."

We found a table and waited for our order. Across from me, behind Beth's head was a mural of a swimming pool in the middle of a desert in which the Beatles, Marilyn Monroe, Pope John Paul, Einstein, Beetlejuice, and others cavorted. I couldn't help staring. And smiling. Beetlejuice especially pleased me.

When I tasted my first bite of the pizza, I forgave the Hard Rock Coliseum atmosphere. I grew up in Jersey, dined often in NYC, and attended a college in Chicago, so I know pizza. Experts will tell you that great pizza requires fresh ingredients or perfect crust. No doubt these play a role, but for my money, the real secret is grease. Too little, and there's no flavor; too much and it tastes slimy. Just the right amount of grease and you sing paeans to the god of taste buds. Such was Saggio's. "Sure glad you had a pizza craving."

"I've had a lot of cravings lately," Beth said slyly. "It's usually artichokes and Oreos. No pickles and ice cream yet."

I didn't catch on until the last reference. "You're preggers?" For as long as I'd known Beth, she'd wanted a child. But she was forty-five and single; I thought she'd given up her age-constrained dream.

"Yes, indeed!" she beamed. "I consumed a ton of hormones, and the artificial insemination finally took. My own egg and my step-cousin's sperm."

I glanced up at the mural and looked at Einstein. If Daddy is Mommy's step-cousin, what does that do to the Theory of Relativity? "Well, congratulations! How far along are you?"

"Seventeen weeks. Still early. That's one of the reasons I wanted you on this contract; I want competent people so I can take a day off now and then if I need it. My OB/GYN says any major stress, and I could lose the baby."

"Is it a boy or a girl?" I chewed slowly, prolonging the gustatory ecstasy.

"Don't want to know; I like the suspense." Beth sprinkled grated cheese on what remained of her all-veggie pizza slice. "Have you ever thought about motherhood, Tess?"

The lilt in her voice told me she wanted to "share," but share I couldn't. The idea of an expensive, incontinent mini-me has never held much appeal. Raj is enough of an outlet for my nurturing instincts. "Roark and I talked about it, way back when. But deep down, we both knew I would've made a lousy mother."

"How is Roark these days?"

The gay sailor who had once joined me in a paper marriage to get the Naval Investigative Service off our backs was living contentedly in Maryland. "He's fine; he brags that he's the only guy over forty in the Beltway region without a receding hairline." I drained my ice tea. "I miss him sometimes. We sure had fun back in our NASB days."

"NASB?"

"Naval Air Station, Brunswick." The little base was now closed, a casualty of budget problems. When I was stationed there, NASB had hosted ASW patrol squadrons, a survival school, Navy Exchange, dispensary, JAG office, and commissary, all tucked snugly within the evergreens of coastal Maine. Daily life had been *McHale's Navy* meets *Northern Exposure*, with more lobster traps, fishing trips, and moose sightings than salutes. I braked my skid of reminiscence, and tuned back into Beth. "Will I get started on the project later today?"

She nodded and wrapped two napkins around the half-slice she couldn't finish. "The project requires a Secret clearance. You still hold one, right?"

Maybe they charged for doggie bags. "Yeah, I still hold my dumb-ass clearance."

"What's with the attitude, Tess? Security's no joking matter," Beth said. Her face took on a slight resemblance to Hillary. "I'm a lot more cautious about terrorists than I used to be, especially now that I'm responsible for another life." She caressed her tummy. "I carry a weapon with me at all times. Can't be too careful."

I wondered if all those hormones had affected her usually fine judgment. "That's a bit overboard, don't you think? New Mexico is a poor state with few high profile events or population centers. What would terrorists want out here?"

"Ever hear of Los Alamos?"

"Touché." Couldn't argue with that. Maybe she was right. Just because I think our national security folks focus on the wrong priorities didn't mean there aren't real bad guys out there. "I'll respectfully concede your right to terrorist paranoia," I suggested, "if you'll concede my right to believe that most of what's done—or left undone—in the name of national security is really about power and money. Speaking of which, when's pay day at Bryce?"

Beetlejuice winked at me as we headed out.

Good sport that she is, Beth oriented me with a mini-tour of old Albuquerque, driving past sights like the Indian Cultural Arts Center and San Felipe de Neri Church, and then heading through downtown along old Route 66. By the time we returned to the Bryce office building, it was almost four in the afternoon. As I well knew, many of the programmers would just be warming up.

Software developers are an eccentric lot. They typically keep odd hours, are fascinated by matters that interest no one else on the planet, and breathe freely only in their own subculture where a token ring is not found in a trilogy and Java CUP has nothing to do with Starbucks.

I'm more of a math major who has learned to build databases than I am a true programmer, but I felt right at home in Bryce's geekster cube farm. As we moved through the main office corridor, I heard "overlay the plume dispersion on the topo maps," "Parzen kernel," "XQuery," and "geotiffs" rise from the vicinity of my new coworkers.

To the uninitiated, the language of computer geeks can seem intimidating, but only one kind of programming truly awes me: assembly language. Regular programming languages, like DOS or C++ or Java, are written in ordinary words and phrases. These may sound odd, but at least we recognize them as statements. The circuitry within a computer is an electronic path which only comprehends OFFs and ONs. Assembly language is the go-between—a language written in odd mnemonics to communicate concepts like "violet" or "transubstantiation" to machines that understand only 1's and 0's. Imagine trying to convey Mozart's concerto for clarinet in A to your remote control, using only the positive and negative poles of its battery to do so, and you'll better appreciate assembly language.

Beth dropped me off at an empty cube and I began organizing my work space. Around 6:30, a cloud of chatter drifted my way; folks were taking a break. I grabbed my totem pole coffee mug and introduced myself to a diminutive woman in her twenties walking down the hallway.

She returned the courtesy. "Jeanette Ng. I designed the preliminary relational database."

"You use Boyce-Codd or Third Normal Forms?"

"Both," she answered with enthusiasm. "Come on back to the break room with me and I'll show you around."

We walked into the middle of a bull session about most embarrassing moments. A senior scientific programmer, who I later learned was Garrick Hagopian, was being drawn into the blarney. "Garrick," someone probed, "what's the story you'll never tell your grandkids?"

While Garrick paused to consider, Beth entered the break room and helped herself to bottled water from the fridge.

My impression of Garrick, a handsome, sweet-looking 400-pound teddy bear, was that he didn't drink or smoke, and I was pretty sure he'd never made a lewd remark in his life. I figured his wildest escapade would involve cheese doodles.

Garrick shifted his bulk and looked bemused. "It would've had to have been that time . . . let's see, about '77 or '78 . . . I was in the graduate program at Michigan State. The city of East Lansing and the state of Michigan passed conflicting laws about the legality of fireworks. While the courts were trying to sort it out, chaos reigned—you could buy sparklers at restaurants, mortar tubes at the Laundromat, M-80s at the supermarket. On Saturday nights, the campus sounded like the Tet Offensive." His face took on a strawberry hue. "One morning I woke up sprawled on a couch in the student lounge, half a bottle of vodka in one hand, and a Roman candle stuffed in my boxers. I have *no* recollection of that night whatsoever!"

We were still trying to picture Garrick in his *American Pie* phase when a network administrator, Dan Guerrero, entered the room and snapped his cell phone shut. "Damn!"

"What's up, Dan-o?" Jeanette inquired.

"The wife and I had reservations to visit the Lightning Field this week. I've been looking forward to that for months. But her sister was just in a car accident. She's OK, but she'll be in the hospital a while. We need to stay here and help with her kids."

Suddenly Beth grew animated. "I've wanted to see the Lightning Field ever since I moved here, but could never manage reservations. Would you sell your spot to me?"

Dan looked relieved. "Sure; no problem. We reserved a room for two."

Beth turned to me. "Want to join me? We'll make your New Mexican contract a real adventure!"

"Don't want to sound unappreciative, but what's the Lightning Field?"

"Conceptual art by Walter De Maria. I'm a big fan of his. He placed hundreds of lightning rods out in the desert, in special designs and formations. And it's located in an area that gets lots of lightning storms. There's a cabin where you can stay, you know, safe, indoors, and watch the lightning come down all around you."

"Sounds striking." This could make crazed weasels seem tame.

4

FOREWARNED

"WILL JODIE FOSTER TAP ME on the shoulder and start lecturing?" Beth asked.

"Criminitlies!" I responded, regressing to an expression my Jersey relatives sometimes used. Before us, the National Radio Astronomy Observatory Very Large Array—the huge satellite dishes that Jodie's team used in *Contact*—spanned the horizon. "I didn't know this place was in New Mexico."

"Neither did I, and I live here."

We'd interrupted the drive from Albuquerque once to stop in Socorro at a Mickey D's for fries and facilities. Now that the excitement of the huge astral hearing aids was behind us, only miles of super-sized sky and John Ford locations loomed ahead.

Humans simmering in prenatal hormones rarely make decisions based solely on logic, so I had to ask. "Beth, weather .com predicted a 30-percent chance of thunderstorms near this Lightning Field tonight. Aren't you concerned about staying in a cabin where lightning comes down all around you? I mean, doesn't Dr. Spock prohibit that on page 314 of his Baby Book? I think even *Mr.* Spock frowns on lightning strikes for pregnant Vulcans."

"Tess, I'm not an idiot! The place isn't as dangerous as it sounds. Even though the artist chose an area where lightning is prevalent, only 5 percent of all visitors actually get to see lightning strikes at the field."

I felt a twinge of disappointment and two twinges of relief. "'Lightning Field' is a bit of a misnomer, then, isn't it? Still . . . the literature said the cabin holds six people. We'll be staying out in the middle of nowhere with four complete strangers."

"The Lightning Field attracts educated art lovers. And maybe some nature lovers. Believe me, if I thought we'd be bunking with criminal types, I wouldn't go."

"So we're driving three hours, investing gas, money and time, to spend the night with perfect strangers and *not* see lightning strike these lightning rods?"

Beth grinned. "Oh, it'll be worth it. The artist configured the site to create special visual effects at sunrise and sunset. That's what I want to see." She took a long sip from her bottled water. "Do you know why today is different from any other day?"

"Oh, wait, wait! I heard this one at Passover!"

Beth ignored my attempt at Jewish humor. "It's June 21. Summer solstice. We get the longest chance of the year to watch what happens at sunset."

My linear math major mind wondered if the *latest* sunset also meant the *longest* sunset, but I didn't want to bicker. Argue with a pregnant woman, and it's two against one. Besides, this visual effect aroused my curiosity.

We listened to a Dixie Chicks CD to kill time. About fifty dead ticks later, we pulled into our destination, the town of Quemado—several buildings (half of them boarded up), a phone booth, motel, gas station, café, six trees, asphalt, and gravel. "If they ever want to film a sequel to *Deliverance* . . . " I began.

Beth gave me a playful shove. "There; that's our building." She pointed to a white storefront with a sign in the window: DIA ART FOUNDATION, LIGHTNING FIELD. Our reservation papers stated that all visitors to the Lightning Field must leave their vehicles in Quemado; the Foundation would provide transportation to and from the site. Fortunately, adequate parking space was not a problem in beautiful downtown Quemado.

Nearby several people hovered around the open tailgate of a black GMC Yukon. Not sure if they were townies or Lightning Field folks, Beth and I went inside the building to investigate. The office was empty, except for a table holding a guest book and a supply of registration and release forms. I skimmed the pages of the guest book. Visitors had come from all over the U.S., as well as Oslo, Berlin, Buenos Aires, Cape Town, and Taipei. Something about this place certainly appealed. I picked up a release form and read its main clause:

> In the event of a lightning storm, we advise you to immediately move off of and away from The Lightning Field. It is dangerous to touch the poles at all times; please refrain from doing so. The Field's terrain has been left in its natural state; animal burrows and uneven ground require your careful attention when walking in the vicinity. Although rarely seen, please be aware that wild animals do inhabit the Field. We appreciate your respect of the artistry, the

premises, and other visitors. By signing below, you acknowledge that you have read and agree to the above conditions. Please enjoy your stay.

I translated from lawyer lingo to native New Jersey:

We advise you not to do the very thing you're paying to do. Don't touch anything; don't mess with anything. Watch where you walk. There are coyotes, scorpions, Gila monsters, and snakes out there. Don't piss them off. By signing below, you indicate you're barely of sound mind. Have a nice day.

How were we supposed to "move off of and away from the Lightning Field" if a storm came up? It wasn't like we'd have transportation to go some place safer. For a pregnant woman, Beth sure had a sporting sense of adventure.

In her role as a corporate CIO, Beth has learned to be a great schmoozer. By the time I completed my paperwork, she was chatting up the folks out by the Yukon, whom we now realized were our fellow travelers. Sweating from the summer afternoon heat, I unloaded our bags in honor of her "delicate condition," and locked up the very dusty Silver Bullet. "I promise to wash and wax you when we get back to civilization," I whispered. I could almost hear the car respond, "*If* you get back to civilization!"

Tossing our belongings in the back of the Yukon, I saw a young man in his late twenties, with a compact body and tension in his carriage, try to load a guitar case into the vehicle. His round face, sandy blond crew cut, cocker spaniel eyes, and Cupid lips produced the overall effect of Charlie Brown grown to manhood.

A rugged Hispanic man in a chambray shirt, blue jeans, black kerchief, and a cowboy hat pushed the guitar case away. "No, Señor, no. There are rules. No one can take music to the Lightning Field."

The young man turned toward the bouncy platinum blonde next to him. Her face was adorned with stylishly retro black glasses. She looked pleasant and intelligent, like someone an ad agency would hire for product promotion. They made eye contact, then she lobbied for his cause. "Folks, I'm Kendra Theisman; this is my husband, Lyle. He plays acoustic guitar, mostly folk-rock. Would any of you object to a bit of quiet guitar music at the cabin?"

Since we didn't have the slightest clue what all the fuss was about, everyone apparently felt as I did, which was that guitar music would liven up a place that didn't have TV, radio, or CD players. The Theismans won the issue unanimously.

The Rule Enforcer shrugged and allowed the guitar in the back compartment, muttering, "It's because I'm a substitute driver. They wouldn't pull this shit if Dale were here." He turned to me. "You two goin' to the Lightning Field?"

I nodded. "I'm Tess Camillo; this is Beth Butler. We're using Dan Guerrero's reservations. He had a family emergency."

I expected him to verify this information against an official guest list, but he merely nodded. "I'm Jorge, your driver. We're waiting for one more person, and if he's not here soon, we leave without him." He cleared his throat of dust and apparent misanthropy, and spat on the ground.

Lyle and Kendra were the youngest members of our group and presumably the most spry. Graciously, they accepted the confined space that passed for the rear seat. Beth slid into the middle seat, and I followed. On her opposite side, the door opened and a man climbed in next to her.

Beth introduced us. "Tess, this is Ned Merkur. He's a museum curator from Nevada. Ned, Tess Camillo." We shook hands. What hair Ned had, which wasn't much, was butterscotch in color, and curly. His aquamarine eyes danced with intelligence. I liked him instantly.

The last guest arrived, shutting off the ignition of a late model blue Jetta, and quickly tossing a leather duffle into the Yukon. He climbed on board with athletic grace, taking the front seat next to the driver. He appeared to be in his mid-thirties, about six feet tall, and of mixed Black and Middle Eastern ancestry. He was decked out in L. L. Bean and groomed like a male model. He introduced himself as Rashid Prince, then quietly settled down, as though he were resuming a state of meditation. As we rode, Kendra and Lyle talked in soft buzzy tones with one another in the seat behind us.

We'd gone perhaps twenty miles on a state road that curved like a licorice rope through cattle ranches and parched scrub, when Jorge announced, "Here's where the ride gets interesting!" He turned onto a private road marked only by a mailbox post. Soon we were rattling over ribbed gravel, ruts, and cattle guard bumps while every bolt in the chassis screeched in protest. I delight at the combination of motion and speed, and soon realized that if I positioned myself just right on the seat, the road vibrations added pleasure to the trip, like sitting on a washer during the spin cycle. Beth looked like she was about to have morning sickness in the afternoon.

We'd been swerving through the boonies for another

twenty minutes when a rustic cabin appeared on our right. Jorge pulled onto a dirt path leading to it and parked. Moving together like one organic being, we got out and took a good long look at the enigmatic Lightning Field in front of us. We saw a whole lot of nothing.

5

BEERLY BELOVED

SOMEWHERE OUT THERE in front of us were four hundred lightning rods, but due to a *trompe l'oeil* played by the afternoon light, the poles blended into the landscape so well you could barely see them. When you did spot them, they looked no more glamorous or impressive than dull gray posts. We were underwhelmed.

We turned back toward the cabin, our abode for the night. Its exterior reminded me of a coconut husk—dark brown, natural, and splintery—with a rough shingle roof and in front, the most primitive structure to which you could apply the word "porch." Jorge called it the veranda.

He gave us a guided tour, starting at the front door which opened into the great room. This space featured a wooden dining table and six chairs, a coffee table, three armchairs, and a wood stove. In the ninety-two-degree heat, no one asked about wood for a fire. The all-wood interior held not a rug, pillow, curtain, cushion, or picture to diminish the "Termite's Paradise" effect. The windows lacked curtains, blinds, or drapes, but we knew they held glass because winged critters buzzed against the panes. There were no fans or screen doors, and it was far too hot to leave doors shut, so the interior had a thriving community of flies and wasps to keep the termites from getting lonely. The décor was not without its graces—a bowl of perfect red apples on the dining table welcomed us, and the globe of an antique lantern glistened in the afternoon sun.

Two bedrooms abutted the great room (one with a double bed; one with twins), along with a bathroom, and a tiny space—barely more than a closet—that held an emergency phone. I mentally dubbed that the Bat Cave.

Jorge moved into the kitchen. Opening the fridge, he showed us the baking dish of chile enchiladas the Dia Art Foundation had prepared for us to cook when our internal dinner bells clanged. The fridge also held bacon, eggs, and bread for tomorrow's breakfast. In the intense heat, we were more interested in cold beverages, of which there were none. Zero. Beth had brought a few bottled waters, but otherwise, we were *très sec.*

Jorge then led us through the back door, along a wooden walkway to a third bedroom with twin beds, clearly an add-on with a separate entrance and its own diminutive bath. I expected him to assign quarters: "This is where you'll sleep; here's where you two will be," but nothing was quite that defined at the Lightning Field. Left to sort out our own sleeping arrangements, we quickly agreed to give Lyle and Kendra the front bedroom with the double bed. Beth asked if we could have the add-on bedroom with its own bath, since peeing was one of her favorite pastimes these days. They all smiled broadly when they learned she was preggers, and Ned and Rashid readily accepted the remaining inside bedroom.

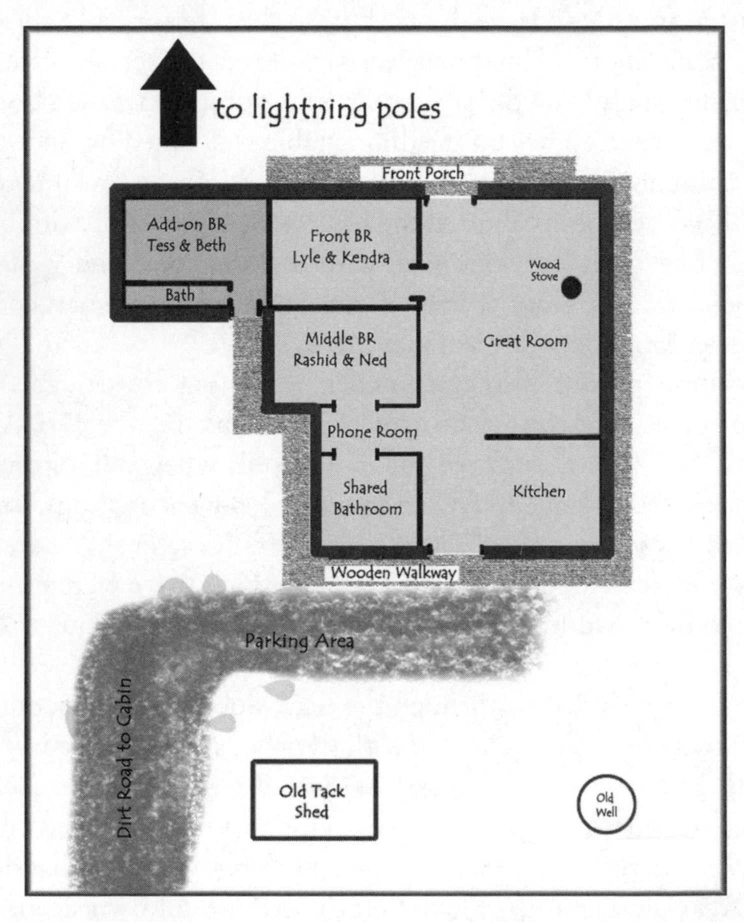

We coerced Jorge into making a beer run for us, then everyone quickly became occupied, flopping suitcases on beds and floors, turning faucets to see if they worked, relieving bladders, or gazing at the Lightning Field. After collecting beer funds, Jorge departed. To give Beth a few moments of restful privacy, I followed Jorge out the back door.

"What's that?" I asked, pointing.

"An old well. Dried up."

"And was that an outhouse?" I indicated a tiny shack nearby.

"Nah, that's an old tack shed, probably full of mice. I gotta go for the beer."

A coconut-shell cabin, a dry well, a decrepit tack shed, and four hundred lightning rods: what had I gotten myself into?

Beth and I cooled down with tap water and read the Visitors Manual, which we found on the great room coffee table. We learned that the lightning poles were fifteen to twenty feet tall. Though the terrain was rough, the poles were arranged so that a sheet of glass placed on their tips would sit evenly. Commendable, if Zeus ever fancies a glass-topped coffee table. My mathematical mind was drawn to the fact that the dimensions of the Field were factors: 4^2 poles by 5^2, to be exact. I liked that.

Lyle and Kendra, undeterred by the heat, set out to walk the circumference of the Lightning Field. Rashid sat on the porch facing the poles, sketching. Ned wandered around outside the cabin with binoculars, examining his new environment. Beth suggested we traverse the thirty-five or so yards between the porch and the nearest pole, to get a closer look. My first box of crayons contained a color called Burnt Sienna, something for which I, as a New Jersey kindergartener, had absolutely no context: it's a Western color. The ground beneath our feet and all around us was burnt sienna. The burnt part seemed apropos, given the area's lightning strikes and scorching sun. Maybe a storm wouldn't be such a bad thing tonight after all; the earth needed the water.

We picked our way through rabbit brush, creosote, coyote scat, bristly grasses, and wildflowers, all of which thrived out here. Go figure.

Beth looked around, making sure we were out of earshot before she spoke. "Tess, I'm not sure I can handle this."

Her voice was shaky. I stopped to examine some petite white daisies with egg yolk centers. "'This' what?"

She nodded toward the cabin where Rashid sat on the porch. "I feel like the most politically incorrect Neanderthal admitting it, but it's freaking me out to have Rashid in our group. I don't believe in stereotyping; you know that, Tess. But my nervous system seems to be functioning on its own." Beth had worked at UCSD for many years, and universities are major proponents of political correctness. I also knew Beth supervised people at Bryce with the surnames Alam, Habib, and Mohammed, and they were very fond of her. I put my arm around my friend's shoulders. "Your hormones are holding your frontal lobes hostage. I haven't seen any 'Seventy-two Virgins Await Me' gleam in Rashid's eye. Why don't you get to know him? Talk with him, and see what happens. After that, if he still rattles your cage, we can ask Jorge to take us back to Quemado when he returns from the beer run."

We started walking again, slowly. Beyond the Field, a low range of indigo mountains chiseled the horizon with their subtle beauty.

Beth sighed. "Oh, I'll settle down. But if there's any sign of trouble, you'll protect me, right?"

"Of course." Me, *in loco parentis*? Or perhaps *paternis.* Criminitlies!

We reached the first pole. Its slender phallic power conjured a warrior's spear, but there was nothing primitive about its shiny stainless steel substance. The resulting effect was simultaneously ancient and ultramodern; a Roman spear built to Romulan specs. Standing among the poles, I gained fresh appreciation for thc artistry of the Lightning Field. No matter where I looked, from whatever direction, each pole was perfectly aligned with others within a mesmerizing grid.

Beth and I meandered to the next nearest pole. A prairie dog sat at its base, guarding a burrow. A few yards away, another prairie dog sniffed the air, probably assessing how much of a bother we were going to be. Beth and I examined a few more poles up close and personal, then Nature tapped Beth on the bladder, and we returned to the cabin.

Beth and I soon joined Rashid and Ned, who were now both on the porch. One of them had freshened up with a very appealing men's cologne.

I whispered to Beth, "I'd french Pat Robertson for a cold beer." I turned toward our fellow travelers on the porch and asked, "Has Jorge come back yet?"

Rashid shook his head *no* and checked his watch. "Not yet."

A jittery Beth approached him and asked about his sketches. I sat down a few feet away near Ned. He wore rumpled khaki shorts, a faded blue U2 tee shirt and sandals. About five-foot-nine, he was built solid and stocky, like me, and looked to be in his fifties. His last name, Merkur, sounded German, but those impish eyes and smile spoke Gaelic to me.

"So you're a museum curator?" I asked, with a covert sniff. He wasn't the one with the quality cologne.

"Yes . . . " he replied with a humorous hesitant inflection that told me there was more in what he didn't say than what he did.

"For an art museum?"

"For the Off the Map Museum in Las Vegas."

I smiled. "OK, you got me. What kind of museum is that?"

"What's 'off the map' is Area 51, the military base where things go on that the government feels its citizens can't know about."

At the word "government," I sensed a tick of interest, a tuning in, on the part of Rashid, though he kept up his conversation with Beth.

"You're curator of an Area 51 museum?" I mirrored to confirm understanding, just like Lee Anne, a therapist I once dated, had taught me.

Ned nodded, clearly enjoying my surprise. "Curator, owner; chief, cook and bottle washer."

Area 51 holds a place of honor in UFO folklore, second only to Roswell. I'd learned quite a bit about it in 1999 when I helped develop an intranet web site for the Nevada Test Site. NTS, situated right next to Area 51, had for decades been an atomic weapons test area. I figured if anything in the vicinity had three arms and an eye in the middle of its forehead, it was more likely to be a human exposed to the Test Site's radioactive contamination than an alien.

Suddenly my eye caught a large animal moseying through the Lightning Field. "Ned, what is that?" I asked, pointing. Ned focused his binoculars on the animal.

"Pronghorn antelope." He handed me the binoculars. The animal was rust and cream in color with striking black facial markings and dark horns. Beautiful. I returned the binoculars.

If I hadn't found Ned appealing, I'd have made a cheap joke about Flying Purple People Eaters and excused myself. But I respected his intelligence. "How did you get involved with Area 51?"

"I'm a vet; I studied veterinary medicine at the University of Illinois. In the '80s, I served as a forensic veterinarian on Project BOVMUT, an FBI investigation into cattle mutilations in Colorado, New Mexico, and Nevada." Ned paused and looked at me, assessing my reaction.

Was it my imagination or was Rashid trying to eavesdrop again? I asked Ned, "What'd you find out?"

"Some of the mutilations could easily be explained by scavengers and other natural occurrences. But only a few. The evidence led us to dismiss the notion that satanic cults were behind the mutilations—they just didn't have the organization, equipment, and other means to pull off something of that scope. And then there were the persistent reports of black helicopters in the areas where the mutilations occurred . . . " Ned sipped a glass of water and seemed to change his mind about something. "Let's just say my conclusions led me to look long and hard at government activities in Area 51. I think the public deserves to know as much as possible about it; thus, the museum."

"So what do you think the government's got up there in Area 51?"

"I *know* what they've got there. The question is, why is the government hiding it from the public?"

6

A JOLT OF SOLSTICE

THE PROBLEM WITH the radical fringe is they're so often right.

Think about it. Goldwater said we wouldn't win in Vietnam unless we nuked 'em. Morality issues aside, he was right in saying we couldn't win with the military tactics we were using. Ralph Nader seemed like a wing nut until seat belts and air bags saved lives. And Congressional records show that Dennis Kucinich was as much a prophet as Isaiah. Visionaries nourish themselves on the future, washing it down with the social bitters of being ahead of their peers.

The government probably was hiding something in Area 51. I doubted it was little green men, but little blue women with intergalactic charge cards were a distinct possibility. I was right on the cusp of learning more Area 51 intrigue when Beth touched me on the shoulder. "I'm hungry; let's cook those enchiladas." She practically dragged me into the kitchen.

Reluctantly I excused myself. Beth retrieved the enchilada dish from the fridge while I pre-heated the oven. Enchiladas, yummer; calories, bummer. Lately I'd been eating as though in prep for an arctic hibernation. I'd had a Big Daddy burger at Boll Weevil, pizza at Saggio's, fries at Mickey D's, and Danishes in the break room at Bryce Corporation. My belly was pooching over my waistband, threatening to push me into an X-rated size. Body fat does not bode well for breast cancer survivors; fat stores estrogen which certain tumors thrive on. Tonight thc only choicc was enchiladas, but I'd soon have to stop lying across the track in front of an oncoming Weight Train. I broke from this Oprahesque self-castigation when I realized Beth was talking to me.

" . . . were right, Tess; he seems OK. His dad was an Army officer stationed in Germany. He met Rashid's mother—she's from Cyprus—when he was on leave. Rashid was born in the States."

I glanced at my watch as I took the enchiladas from Beth and slid them into the oven. 6:15 p.m.

"I like the guy's energy. What's he do for a living? From the way he looks—and smells—I'd say he's a successful architect."

"Sorry, honey, you're off the mark. He's an insurance fraud investigator."

"What's an insurance investigator doing out here?" I asked as I futzed around the kitchen, shooing flies and discovering what was stored where. Beth found the percolator and decided to brew some coffee. At least it would be a change from tap water.

"He's been taking an art class at night. His instructor mentioned the Lightning Field in a lecture, and Rashid got curious. It doesn't rattle me to be around him now; I've calmed down," she assured me. "Besides, I remembered that I brought my self-defense weapon with me."

Damn, I'd forgotten she was going through life with weapons as well as with child. Suddenly I felt a lot *less* safe. "What are you totin', anyway? Pepper spray?"

Beth located the pot holders and laid one by the stove for future use. "Pepper sprays are notoriously unreliable. I bought myself a Taser C2, a stun gun powerful enough to knock someone off their feet, if necessary."

I didn't anticipate anyone needing such electric comeuppance. "Speaking of protective measures, check this out." I lifted the lid of a built-in storage cabinet next to the stove. Inside were trail mix snacks, condiments, utensils, silverware, and dishes. "See this metal lining? They're keeping it safe from mice." I refrained from adding "rats or roaches."

Beth gave a little shudder. "I could've lived without that news flash, Tess," she replied and went off to our private potty.

Kendra and Lyle returned from their walk around the Field and settled on the porch. I studied them with a mixture of joy and envy. They touched each other easily and often. She would fall into his chest, laughing; he would rumple her hair affectionately. When he was near her, he beamed; if she stepped away, he reverted to the cautious Charlie Brown, wary of what the world could inflict. She was the extrovert; he the introvert, but it was evident they both got something they needed from one another.

I decided to get to know my fellow cabin dwellers better. "What kind of work do you do?"

Kendra answered for them. "I teach printmaking at the University of New Mexico's Art Department. Lyle owns a bike shop near the campus—plenty of student business." She patted his hand affectionately.

"She does a lot more than teach printmaking," Lyle interjected. He told his wife, "Tell her about all your volunteer work."

Like the sun and moon, Kendra beamed with the pride Lyle reflected back to her. She shrugged. "It's only two evenings a week. I volunteer with the Albuquerque school district's special ed students. Sometimes it's more rewarding than my real job."

"So your interest in art must be what brought you to The Lightning Field?" I asked.

Again, Kendra responded for them. "I'd never heard of Walter De Maria's earthworks until we moved to New Mexico, but of course, once I did, I couldn't wait to see it."

We all matched our gaze to her desire, and looked out again on the field of poles.

6:25 p.m.

The angle of the sun was changing; the solstice sunset had begun. The lightning rods now emerged visually, their bright metallic lines, disparate elements introduced by a New York artist to this natural New Mexican plain. Anticipatory adrenaline began to bond our little group.

That bond was still forming when we heard the rumble of a vehicle on the road leading to the cabin. Certain that it was Jorge with the beer, several of us cut through the great room and kitchen to meet him out back. Instead we saw an official-looking truck, not the Yukon.

"Looks like a sheriff or something," Ned observed. "Wonder what's up?"

Beth looked somewhat pointedly at Rashid and said, "They probably swing by to check on visitors and make sure everything's OK."

The truck pulled up the cabin driveway and a park ranger got out. He walked like he'd just dismounted a horse instead of an F-150. Close to retirement age, he had a cleft in his chin, making him look like Kirk Douglas in a *Gunsmoke* cameo.

"Sorry to intrude, folks. I'm George Calvert, ranger up at the Cibola National Forest. Is this everybody in your group?"

We looked around and realized Lyle and Kendra had remained on the porch. "There are two more of us over here," Rashid answered and led the way to the porch where we disrupted some conjugal groping.

Ranger Calvert addressed us all. "I felt it was important to stop by and let you Lightning Field visitors know—there's been an increase in mountain lion sightings lately."

Oh, goodie; now Beth could be paranoid about terrorists *and* wildlife.

The ranger continued, "There've been three sightings in the past week at the Navajo Reservation just north of here, so please be careful. You know what to do if you see one?"

"Try to look big," I suggested. You learn a lot about mountain lions if you live in San Diego County.

"Right. Raise your hands in the air; stand on a rock; whatever. Mountain lions, or cougars, as we sometimes call 'em, are wary about attacking anything that might turn out to be a larger predator. Best thing you can do, of course, is just be on the alert, OK?"

"It was nice of you to stop by and warn us," Beth said. "Would you like some coffee? I just brewed a pot."

Calvert smiled. "I could use a cup; thanks."

When Beth returned with it, we all found a space on the now-crowded "veranda" and gazed at the glistening poles in the Field.

6:37 p.m.

The evening brought relief from the heat; even the flies seemed less pesky. As far as we could see lay a vast expanse of high desert. "It feels like I could tuck my entire home state of New Jersey into these open spaces," I remarked.

"I'm a city girl," said Kendra. "Grew up in downtown St. Louis. When I was a kid, my folks took me camping along the Illinois River at a state park. It always seemed like a whole other world!"

Rashid joined in. "Wish my son liked camping. He's only eight, but he gets bored outdoors." He flashed beautiful white teeth in a rueful smile. "Kids today prefer video games and Ipods."

"When I was young, we never got bored with camping," offered the ranger. "There was always something to do. Dig for worms. Fish. Climb trees. Catch fireflies. And when it got dark, there were the tales around the campfire, just to keep things interesting."

Ned agreed. "Sure; ghost stories, horror tales, folklore—I remember them well. The older scouts in my troop once convinced me we were camping on an Indian graveyard."

"They told me potato eyes would turn into cat's eye marbles if you soaked them in Coke," Kendra shared. "I tried it once when I was camping. Needless to say, all I got were soggy spud eyes." She giggled.

"Our prevailing camp myth was that the Jersey Devil ate spider cocoons washed down with Fizzies," I contributed.

Lyle looked like he was about to barf, and Ned seemed nonplussed. Maybe he'd never heard of the Jersey Devil and thought I was from one of those satanic cults he'd investigated. Or maybe he'd never heard of Fizzies, a tablet-based effervescent soft drink of my youth.

Ranger Calvert had just started to excuse himself when Kendra spoke again. "Lyle sleeps so sound . . . " she began. Lyle's eyes went to hers and pleaded, but Kendra proceeded anyway, " . . . that when he went camping, the kids used to dip his hand in water and make him wet his sleeping bag. He still sleeps like the dead. If we do get thunder and lightning tonight, he'll doze right through it."

There were a few uncomfortable chuckles. Lyle looked down. The guy had gorgeous thick eyelashes.

Beth checked her watch: 6:45 p.m. "Time to get those enchiladas out of the oven," she announced.

The ranger took his leave. No sooner did his truck pull away than we heard Jorge arrive. The next few moments were a blissful blur of icy bottles and snapping caps.

"What happened, Jorge? We thought you forgot us," I said, offering a euphemism for, "we thought you'd ripped us off and we'd never see you or our money again."

"Hey, I had to pick up my daughter from school, pick my wife up from work, and run a couple of my own errands. And I was hungry; I ate dinner before I came back out."

"Well, thanks for doing this." Ned raised a bottle of Bud. "You really saved our butts."

Jorge soon climbed back into his vehicle, ready to head out. I saw Ned go over and talk to him through the SUV window.

He pulled a wad of cash from his wallet and gave it to Jorge, and the Yukon departed.

With frosty beer and hot enchiladas, we were set for dinner. Again we congregated on the porch, juggling warm plates, napkins, forks, and cold brews. None of us used the indoor dining table; no one wanted to miss a moment of the light show unfolding before us.

7:15 p.m.

We finished our meals—forks no longer clanged; plates no longer clattered. It was so quiet we could hear rabbits scamper. The lightning rods now stood like the Chinese terra cotta warriors that watch over Shaanxi province. But these four hundred sentinels were not terra cotta—they were slivers of silvery gold—and their contrast with the earth grew more vivid with each change of the sun's angle. We watched the glow of the poles intensify, observing something none of us had ever seen before.

7:40 p.m.

Creosote and desert sage scented the air. Purple clouds skirted the distant mountains. The sky deepened to the color of a blue jay and the rods shimmered with a rosier gold. The poles that had appeared so disparate with nature a little while ago now seemed in sync with their surroundings.

At different times Ned, Rashid, and I walked around to the rear of the cabin to absorb the stillness of the terrain before coming back into view of the Field. Intuitively we gave each other space, affording opportunities for solitude. I spotted another antelope grazing; I could see why mountain lions found the area inviting. From time to time, each of us wandered out into the Lightning Field, awestruck by its evanescent beauty. Eventually we all returned to the porch.

The spell was temporarily broken when Jorge once again pulled up. Ned ran out to meet him. A moment later, Jorge departed and Ned came back with a bottle of twenty-year-old Scotch. "Should've thought of this the first time, but better late than never," Ned said. "Please join me if you'd like."

Beth declined due to her pregnancy; Ned poured shots for the rest of us.

8:36 p.m.

The sky darkened a few more degrees to deep slate blue. Time bent; we spoke in murmurs. Four hundred grand filaments of coppery neon rose erect from the ground. It was as though Mother Earth had exposed her own nerve fibers—not painfully, but in a holy, mystical unveiling—and we were privy to this intimate rite. Slowly the poles' incandescence dulled from fiery copper to an amber burnish, the color of the whiskey in our glasses. "This was worth the trip," I whispered to Beth.

In reverential silence we watched the dying of the light.

7

JOT OR TITTLE

THE DARK, FLY-INFESTED bathroom which Beth and I shared was big enough for a jot or a tittle, but not both. Nevertheless, it served its primary purpose. I allowed it to serve that purpose for me shortly after nightfall.

On my way back to the great room where we were all socializing, I used the walkway to the kitchen door. Swallows fluttered in their nests under the eaves. At least I hoped they were swallows. To the east, stars offered twinkling eye-candy, but to the west, ominous clouds obscured the night sky, and dampness now hung in the air.

Lyle was playing his guitar when I rejoined the group. Kendra sat at his feet on a big pillow she had brought with her. Ned, Rashid, and I found space at the dining room table, while Beth rested in an arm chair near the wood stove. I selected an apple from the bowl on the table and kept the doctor away while I listened.

Lyle was a decent guitarist with a rich tenor voice. As he finished the last stanza of Coheed & Cambria's "The Light and the Glass," I saw a hint of petulance in Kendra's expression, perhaps because her introverted Significant Other was receiving all of the attention.

We were a subdued sextet, content to have Lyle's gentle tunes re-ground us after our ethereal solstice experience. Ned seemed withdrawn, lost in his own thoughts or in the effects of twenty-year-old Scotch. There'd be time enough at breakfast tomorrow to quiz him about Area 51. Beth fought the yawns. Today's adventure had exhausted her. Rashid acted like a documentary filmmaker, aloof and observant, contributing little but taking everything in. This trait probably made him a good fraud investigator. When Lyle finished the song, we encouraged an encore.

"OK, one more song, but then I've gotta call it quits. We're getting up early to catch the poles at sunrise." Lyle tuned two strings and cleared his throat. "This one seems fitting. It's called 'The Ballad of Casey Deiss.' My dad sang it to me when I was little; it was one of his favorites." Lyle finger-picked the intro and began singing.

Casey had a mark of simple value
He had a star between his eyes
In his hands he held an axe blade
The Greek symbol of thunder and fire.

On a night when the heavens were crying
He went out and took his blade
Chopping wood to warm his hearthside
The lightning came and my brother died.

Potent minor chords, slick with honeyed melancholy, transfixed us: we felt for this mysterious man struck down by lightning. Lyle tucked the guitar into its case. We said goodnight and headed to our rooms.

Beth and I washed up, got into our jammies, and slipped between crisp white sheets. Our twin beds lay parallel to one another on either side of the room. The head of each bed faced the front of the cabin, with windows looking out toward the Lightning Field. Two beds, a night stand with towels and lamp, and a wash basin were crammed into the tiny room like Michael Jordan in a Mini Cooper. As I lay in bed with my head on the pillow, the cabin walls were only inches from my face. I tried to relax, willing myself a voyage to Nod. Beth tossed and turned.

Outdoors, the silence had soothed me. The absence of ringing phones, traffic, and constant chatter appealed. Contrasting with that, I discovered, was the noise level indoors. Every time someone moved, floorboards creaked. The walls had no insulation, and with no outdoor background noise, nothing prevented interior sounds from registering throughout the cabin. Though separated from the others by the cabin's layout, Beth and I could hear every hiccup, flush, and fart; every moan on every mattress. True privacy was a scarce commodity at the Lightning Field.

Eventually I got used to the floor board squeaks and tuned them out. The only sound that continued to disturb me was the termites: I thought I could hear them chewing the walls. My brain's sleep center found that unsettling. I had a long talk with my sleep center that went like this:

Me: "The termites are more interested in these delectable wooden walls than in crawling under your sheets. Just go to sleep."

SC: “Yes, but they’re so close! How can I ignore that sound?”

(burp, floorboard squeak, flush)

Me: “How do you ignore all those other noises?

SC: “I don’t know. They’re just normal noises. I’m not *used to* hearing termites near my pillow.”

Me: “OK, try this. Imagine designing a database that would detect patterns in termite activity.”

SC: “Damn. Crazy as that sounds, it might work.”

It did. I’m not sure when Beth drifted off, but I was soon sawing wood faster than the termites could chew it.

8

BLINDED BY THE LIGHT

I WAS AWAKENED BY a roaring Tyrannosaurus brandishing a whip.

Trembling, I sat up and looked around. Beth was awake, too. We kneeled on our beds and looked out the windows toward the Field. BBs of rain pelleted the window panes and roof. Thunder shook the cabin, and masterful spikes of tortured electrons thrust into the ground.

A lightning bolt is hotter than the sun. Yes, hotter than the nuclear star that warms our planet. The energy contained in a sizable thunderstorm is greater than the energy expended in an atomic bomb, like those detonated at the Nevada Test Site. Unlike our ancestors, we're rarely in close proximity to such primal power. Those who watched Mt. St. Helens blast brimstone, those who saw the 2004 tsunami crash ashore, Katrina victims who watched as their homes were ripped away—such people know moments when the Voice out of the Whirlwind does not sing a lullaby.

I watched the lightning lash and lick the Field, too fascinated by the primacy of its power not to. I turned to Beth. "Looks like we get to be one of the lucky 5 percent."

She cringed as thunder boomed again. "Be careful what you wish for."

We could hear the voices and movement of our fellow visitors on the other side of the wall. To join them, we'd have to run outside through the downpour in our pajamas. We decided our seats in the loge were just fine; we didn't need to move to the orchestra section.

One bolt landed between the cabin and the Field. Too close. Way too close. I should've blinked, but my reactions weren't quick enough: lightning travels faster than humans blink. The intensity of the flash blinded me. Had I been permanently "blinded by the light"? No, please, God, I don't want to be another runner in the night, stumbling through a private darkness. For several eternal seconds I blinked, willing my tears to restore my vision. Gradually, mercifully, my sight returned.

By the time the thunderstorm passed, the electrical charge in the air was palpable. It made me feel weak down to a somatic, cellular level. Beth peed once more for good measure, then we both slid under our covers, seeking the safer realm of dreams.

9

NOT MR. BODDY

I AWOKE AT 5:40 A.M. to a tug on my pajama sleeve. At first I thought the termites were being playful, but soon realized the tugger was Beth.

"If you want to see the sunrise effect on the poles, you'd better get up! Coffee's on in the kitchen."

I'd support any referendum that prohibited vociferous enthusiasm before 7:00 a.m., but I grew less resentful when I remembered that of all the gin joints in all the world, a solstice sunrise was appearing in mine.

Beth took a handful of Oreos from a tote bag and headed for the kitchen. I hauled my butt out of bed, performed hasty ablutions, and donned jeans, tee shirt, and sneakers. I don't remember brushing my hair, but I didn't hear Beth gasp when I entered the kitchen, so I probably did.

Ned and Rashid were already on the front porch, mainlining Yuban. Both were fighting sleep deprivation or mild hangovers. I watched steam rise from their coffee cups into the brisk morning air.

The sun was up high enough for the first poles to emerge as glistening slivers in the pink dawn, but the temperature was in the low fifties. I shivered. Was this the same Lightning Field where I had sweltered? Everything seemed different. Yesterday the ground had been desiccated and crunchy; now it was caked and muddy. Angles seemed harsher; corners less rounded. Even the smells had changed; the sun hadn't yet warmed the plant resins that would scent the air.

I filled a coffee mug and helped myself to trail mix from the mice-proofed cabinet. None of us felt inclined to Hop Sing bacon, eggs, and toast at this hour. When Beth headed for our bathroom, I headed for the porch. I noticed the front bedroom door was still closed. "Aren't Kendra and Lyle getting up?" I asked Ned and Rashid. "I thought they wanted to watch the sunrise."

Rashid yawned and stretched. "Haven't seen them yet. None of us got much sleep last night, what with the storm and all. Maybe they changed their minds and decided to sleep in."

"Or maybe," added Ned impishly, "they're waiting for the rest of us to leave so they can have a little privacy." On that note, he and Rashid departed for a stroll through the poles on the left side of the Field.

Beth and I set out toward the poles directly in front of the cabin, like we had the day before. Our path took us within thirty feet of the burnt-earth scar where lightning had struck near the cabin.

We hadn't even reached the first pole when a darting coyote drew our attention.

"Did you see that?" I asked Beth.

"Just barely. They sure are quick."

"He's probably chasing rabbits." I looked ahead in the vicinity from which the coyote had appeared. Something lay on the ground two lightning poles away. I nudged Beth and pointed. It looked like a body. Mr. Boddy in the Lightning Field with a cactus spine? We halted in the middle of the mud and rabbit brush. "Go back to the cabin and wait."

Beth just stood there.

"You asked me to help watch out for you. For your own sake and the sake of that little chitlin you're carrying, go back to the cabin and wait. Now!" Her hormones turned on the tear faucet, but she started for the cabin. I moved ahead.

There are legends around the world about what it means to die by lightning. A special blessing of God, some say, while others deem it a curse. Not many cultures are neutral about the way life was scorched out of Kendra Theisman.

The ground beneath her was charred. She lay on her back, her corn silk hair flung around her face. For the first time I got a look at her without the retro glasses. She had a clear complexion and naturally arched brows. She was—or had been—quite an attractive young woman, but there was now a waxy sheen to her skin. Ants crawled near her eyelids, and in and out of her nose and mouth. Her pajama top was partially open and an odd burn wound was evident directly over her heart. Between her pajama top and bottoms, the flesh beneath her right rib cage was exposed. The coyote, an opportunistic feeder, had discovered that vulnerable area.

I put my fingers on her carotid artery and detected no pulse. I'd seen dead bodies before, and believe me, I far prefer live ones—the livelier, the better, especially those of the female persuasion. I felt lightheaded from the lack of sleep and food, and from prolonged leaning over the body. At least I told myself that's why I felt woozy.

I straightened up and yelled as loudly as I could in Ned and Rashid's direction. "Help! Hey! Over here!" I waved my arms like a ref stung by killer bees. Rashid and Ned came running. Back at the cabin, Beth stood in the doorway. I put my hand out in a "Stop" fashion to deter her from joining us.

Why in hell had Kendra wandered into the Lightning Field in the middle of a fierce lightning storm? And barefoot, in her pajamas? Hadn't she read her visitors registration with its dire caveats? Ned and Rashid had been with her and Lyle in the main part of the cabin during the storm. Surely they would have some information. And Lyle . . . was he still catching z's while his wife lay struck by Zeus' bolt?

Rashid arrived first and quickly took in the scene. His eyes asked me a question; I shook my head no.

Moments later Ned arrived. Immediately he knelt by Kendra's body and began mouth-to-mouth resuscitation, perhaps a knee-jerk response from his veterinary medical training. Within seconds, he stood up, spitting ants and wiping his mouth. "Too late," he whispered.

"You two were with them last night during the storm. Didn't you warn her not to go out in the Lightning Field? Didn't her husband say anything?" I asked.

"Kendra was in the great room with us, yes," said Rashid. "But Lyle slept through the whole thing. And she never said a word about going outside while I was there."

"Rashid's right. We all watched the storm together, but when it subsided, we headed back to our room," confirmed

Ned. "I assumed she went to bed, too, although come to think of it, she was still sitting by the wood stove when I turned in."

The three of us gathered our thoughts, while full daylight obliterated the sunrise glow. The play of the rising sun on four hundred stainless steel rods had lost its thrill.

Rashid took command. "I'll stay here with the body. You two go back and call 911 from that emergency phone."

"No, no one should be left alone with the body," I countered. "If there's anything fishy about her death, there'll be an investigation and. . . ."

Until then it hadn't consciously occurred to me that this was anything other than an unfortunate accident, but something about the scene didn't feel right. Maybe it was that her feet, while not pristine, looked too clean for someone who walked out here in a rainstorm. My doubt found its voice. "How about if we all go back to the cabin together and take turns keeping an eye on the body using your binoculars, Ned? That way no one can mess with anything, but we can make sure coyotes and vultures don't disturb. . . ."

Ned nodded. "My binoculars are at your disposal."

The three of us picked our way through the mud and brush back to the cabin. Rashid went to the Bat Cave to make the call. Beth collared me. "What's going on?"

She took the news surprisingly well, given her enceinte endocrine system.

Rashid returned from the Bat Cave. "They're on their way."

"We have to tell Lyle," said Beth, shifting into trial maternal mode, ready to comfort and console.

Ned retrieved his binoculars and settled on the porch for the first shift of the corpse-watch, thus exempting himself from the onerous duty of breaking the bad news.

Rashid looked at me and Beth. "I'll wake him up, but you two tell him, OK?"

We agreed, and he knocked hard on the front bedroom door. No response. Kendra hadn't been kidding when she said the man slept like the dead. As soon as "like the dead" popped into mind, I had to see what was behind that door. Rashid must've felt the same way, because he turned the knob and went inside without waiting for a response. Beth and I hovered in the doorway, looking away, in case Lyle wasn't dressed. We heard voices, and soon Rashid came out of the room with his arm over the shoulder of a rumpled Charlie Brown in pajamas.

The first words out of Lyle's mouth were the last ones we wanted to deal with: "Where's Kendra?"

At that moment, I really wished the victim had been Mr. Boddy.

10

INNOCENT PANCAKE TURNERS

IN HIGH DESERT AND LOW SPIRITS, we waited for the authorities to arrive. As much to help ground Lyle as to assuage any collective hunger, Ned asked him to help fix breakfast. The normally tantalizing smell of bacon filled the cabin, but our appetites were dim. Even coffee is hard to swallow when downed with sorrow. Still in his pajamas, Lyle ate a bite of toast and pushed his eggs around. Eventually he excused himself, retreated to his room and curled up in a fetal position on his bed. Ned, Rashid, and I ate in shifts and continued to keep watch over Kendra's body. It proved necessary. Twice we had to shoo buzzards from the area.

The heat was rapidly gaining on the day when a blue Ford Expedition and a small white van pulled up, one behind the other. Catron County Sheriff Jett Garcia, a slender six-footer in black Wranglers, a gray and black uniform shirt, and a black ball cap, emerged from the Ford, along with a deputy in similar garb. The sheriff's confident, straightforward demeanor said "competent guy" but his watery eyes and runny nose screamed "allergy attack." He carried a wad of tissues in one hand and showed his ID badge with the other as he introduced himself and his young deputy, Mike Pino, a Native American. If silence is golden, Mike was a walking Fort Knox.

A rotund blonde in her forties stepped out of the van and joined us. Sheriff Garcia introduced her as Dr. June Spiegel, the Field Deputy Medical Investigator. Except for Lyle, who remained curled on his bed, we introduced ourselves.

"Which of you found the body?" Sheriff Garcia wanted to know.

I raised my coffee mug in greeting. "I did."

"Then why don't you take us to it? Deputy Mike will stay with y'all and get your names and contact information."

After giving my info to the deputy, I led the sheriff and Dr. Spiegel to Kendra's body. As they examined the scene, I stood off at a distance, gazing at the enigmatic grid of poles. They thought I was out of earshot, but in the quiet desert their words carried easily.

Dr. Spiegel spoke up. "This doesn't look like a lightning strike to me, Jett."

"What's off?" sniffled the Sheriff.

"Look at her feet. No sane person would walk out here barefoot, especially at night. And if a lightning bolt had struck her while she was walking, the electrical charge would ground itself to the earth. Her feet would be scorched. There's not a mark on them. In fact, there's not even much dirt on them."

My suspicious inklings had been twinkling in the right direction.

Spiegel circled the body again. "Sometimes lightning causes the body's moisture to expand quickly, which splits open clothing, but not the way this pajama top is torn. Her hair's not singed. Her clothes aren't wet. And see this scorch mark on her chest? It's all wrong. This looks like it was made by some kind of tool or instrument."

"Ah, crap." Sheriff Garcia glanced back at the cabin and shook his head. "You thinking homicide?"

"I am, but the autopsy will tell us definitively." She stood up straight and surveyed the area. "First time I've been out here at the Lightning Field. Strange place."

He squinted into the nexus of poles. "Time of death?"

In my peripheral vision, I saw the doctor poking and prodding what used to be Kendra. She looked at her watch. "It's about eight-forty now? Rigor has set in. As a preliminary guess, I'd say somewhere between two-thirty and four-thirty in the morning."

"Can you tighten that window?" he pushed.

"Not until the autopsy."

"OK, I'll send Mike out here to take photos of the scene, and he'll help you load the body." Sheriff Garcia motioned me back to the cabin and blew his nose. Dr. Spiegel stayed with the corpse.

The sheriff roused Lyle and gathered us all together. "The Field Investigator hasn't determined the cause of death, but it don't appear consistent with lightning. Achoo! Mike, you got everyone's name and contact info?"

Mike handed him several pages of notes.

The sheriff addressed his deputy. "Get the camera and take crime scene photos. June's gonna need some help with the body, too."

Mike set off wordlessly to accomplish his tasks. Law enforcement resources out here were a far cry from TV's CSI. Sheriff Garcia found the Dia Art Foundation's phone number in the Visitors' Manual, and went to the Bat Cave to make a call. Apparently even sheriff's cell phones don't work at the Lightning Field. He returned to the great room several minutes later. "Dia gave me permission to search the premises. I need a statement from each of you. No more conversation till I got everyone's statement. You can stay anywhere inside the cabin, or you can walk around outside—just don't go too far. But no talking. Clear?"

We affirmed our understanding, with varying degrees of reluctance. At this rate I might never learn what the government had out in Area 51.

Sheriff Garcia continued, "After I take your statement, I'd like permission to search your personal belongings as well. OK, who wants to go first?"

Rashid volunteered. Leave it to an insurance guy to suck up. Or maybe, being part Arab, he wanted to dispel suspicion right away. He and Sheriff Garcia spoke quietly on the porch as he gave his statement. Much as I tried, I couldn't figure out how to eavesdrop without being conspicuous. I did sneak a peek when the sheriff left the porch for the middle bedroom, where he searched Rashid's leather duffel and other possessions.

Apparently finding nothing noteworthy, the sheriff thanked Rashid for his cooperation and asked, "Would you call the number for 'Dale' posted in the phone room and ask for Jorge Mantilla? The regular Lightning Field guide, Dale, is out of town on vacation. Dia says this Jorge fellow is filling in for him. Tell Jorge that you Lightning Field folks won't be leaving at the normal time, and that he needs to bring more food and drink out here."

"How much longer are you going to keep us here?" I asked, voicing our common concern.

"Tell him I need *bottled* water," Beth interjected. "I don't like to risk faucet water. And orange juice would be good—something healthy."

The sheriff gave Rashid an "ignore the princesses" look and nudged him toward the Bat Cave.

Deputy Mike and Dr. Spiegel loaded Kendra's body into the back of the van, for eventual transport to Albuquerque where (I later learned) all New Mexico autopsies are conducted. Dr. Spiegel departed.

In the great room, the sheriff took my statement next. He pressed me about whether I'd noticed any footprints at the scene before Ned and Rashid arrived. I hated to admit it, but I hadn't noticed—I'd been too focused on Kendra.

Rashid interrupted us to tell the sheriff that after three attempts, he still couldn't reach Jorge. There was no answer at Dale's number.

Sheriff Garcia searched my belongings, and for once I was glad to be traveling *sans* sex toys. While he rummaged, I worked a Sudoku puzzle. I missed my Tinker Toys; I love fidgeting with them. Connecting the colorful wooden rods and spools calms my nerves and helps me think, but I'd left them in San Diego. When I use my Tinker Toys, I crawl around on the floor, hook pieces together, chase round pegs that roll under furniture, and try different configurations. Number puzzles like Sudoku filled the same purpose mentally, but lacked the physical component that helps dissipate tension.

I had just figured out that row five, column four had to be either a two or an eight when Garcia finished going through my things and said he'd interview Beth next. "What are you allergic to, Sheriff?" I asked, trying to build rapport.

"Rodents—mice, gophers, prairie dogs. And their feces." He glanced around the less than sterile cabin, rolled his afflicted eyes, and smiled. "Ain't exactly the Ritz-Carlton, is it?"

"Have you tried allergy pills?"

"I'm on duty. Can't take anything that makes me drowsy," he bemoaned.

I made simpatico noises to the sheriff and interceded on Beth's behalf. "My friend Beth, the woman you're about to question? She's pregnant. If she seems overly emotional about anything, I hope you'll take that into consideration."

"I'll keep it in mind."

He was true to his word. I stayed in our room to give Beth silent support, and watched him search her belongings. He managed to strike an appropriate balance between legal thoroughness and human courtesy. Then he found the Taser.

"Well, I'll be damned. A Taser C2. These babies put out fifty-thousand volts." He turned the five-inch stun gun over in his hand. "This belong to you?"

"Yes; I carry it for, you know, self-defense," Beth answered. I could tell she was nervous from the red flush near her Eve's apple.

Garcia questioned her at length about where and when she bought it and if she'd ever used it. Beth grew more jittery throughout the interview until she made a mad dash for our tiny bathroom. The sheriff and I heard retching. Anxiety and morning sickness are an ugly combination.

Garcia turned to me. "You and Ms. Butler slept in this room last night, right?"

"Right."

"Could anyone have come in and taken that Taser out of your friend's suitcase?"

"After we went to bed, probably not. But someone could've taken it before we turned in."

"Who else in the cabin knew she had a Taser?"

I thought long and hard, but couldn't think of anyone to whom Beth had confided her paranoia or who had overheard our conversation about the weapon.

To his credit, the sheriff simply bagged the Taser, made notes, and continued his interviews and searches. He told Deputy Mike to search the cabin and its surroundings, looking for objects that could've inflicted Kendra's wounds and to note anything unusual or out of place. Mike first headed for the outbuildings—the dry well and tack shed. I followed him from a distance, watching.

When he returned empty-handed, I wandered toward the lightning rods, looking out over blue sky and sienna earth. My chest ached. It took me a few seconds to identify the feeling: I missed Lana. Fiercely. I longed for her fragile, Finnish, fractured-fairy-tale perspective. I longed for the embrace of her hugs, for the silly spats over shelf space in the fridge or whose turn it was to clean the dog poop from the back yard. And I was homesick for San Diego—for the fresh coastal breeze and zippy freeways, for palm trees silhouetted by a Pacific sunset. I didn't just want to leave the Lightning Field; I wanted to see Lindbergh Field. I wanted to go home. Of course, the sheriff was not apt to send us home at that particular moment.

When I returned to the cabin he had already searched Lyle's room, an effort which apparently yielded nothing of interest, and was now in Ned and Rashid's room searching Ned's gear. I visited the kitchen frequently, trying to eavesdrop. I learned that Ned had brought a veterinarian's medical bag with him; he said he traveled with it out of habit. In it, Sheriff Garcia found an electrical cauterization pen which he confiscated. I heard Ned say it was a standard vet's instrument, used mainly after castrations. I could almost see the sheriff's wince.

By the time we'd all given statements and had our possessions searched, deputy Mike had completed his perusal of the premises. He'd been thorough—I'd even seen him check inside the pot-belly stove pipe. All he'd come up with were a few kitchen implements. He'd bagged them on the theory that someone could have heated a spatula or potato masher, then taken Kendra into the kitchen to scald her chest with it. I suppose Mike was trying to be thorough, but I looked upon the bagging of innocent pancake turners with skepticism. A heated kitchen tool could possibly inflict a burn wound, but it wouldn't have killed Kendra. And what would have kept her from screaming? Even with a hand over her mouth, there would have been a scuffle. How could such baneful deeds be accomplished in a cabin where every whisper could be heard through the walls?

A little after one in the afternoon, Sheriff Garcia and Mike wrapped things up, and offered us a ride back to Quemado. The tension inside the crowded SUV was thick enough to make us itch. We weren't stupid. Each of us realized that if Kendra's death was not an accidental lightning strike, then one of us was most likely a killer. And there were only so many of us.

Sheriff Garcia was thinking: I got a damned homicide on my hands.

Rashid was thinking: It's either Tess, Beth, Ned, or Lyle.

Ned was thinking: It's either Tess, Beth, Lyle, or Rashid.

Lyle was thinking: It's either Tess, Beth, Rashid, or Ned.

I was thinking: It's either Ned, Rashid, or Lyle.

Beth was thinking: breast or bottle?

11

SEAL OF SOCORRO

BEAUTIFUL DOWNTOWN Quemado was just as we'd left it about twenty-four hours ago. Seemed like a lifetime. For Kendra, it was.

Sheriff Garcia shepherded us into the Dia Art Foundation office, then issued an APB on the Lightning Field's substitute driver, Jorge Mantilla, and made other phone calls out of earshot. Eventually he addressed us. "Since we don't know the cause of Mrs. Theisman's death, the medical investigator in Albuquerque will have to do an autopsy. Whether accident or homicide, from this point on, the District Attorney's office in Socorro will handle the investigation. None of you are in any kind of official custody, not yet, anyway, so don't give me a reason to change my mind, OK?"

Our heads bobbed up and down like hula dolls on a dashboard.

Sheriff Garcia reached into the pocket of his black denims and pulled out several business cards. "Some time within the next forty-eight hours, you are to report to the DA's Investigator for an interview. Here's the address in Socorro and the phone number." He distributed the cards, then cut us loose.

The sweet relief of not being held in custody inspired me to sail along I-60 at eighty-five miles per hour. We zoomed past a cattle ranch. Most of the cows were a rich mahogany color with creamy spots, although at that speed, the spots do tend to blur. I rolled down the window for fresh air and was reminded where manure comes from.

My mind spun almost as fast as my Pirellis. "I wonder why Ned gave Kendra mouth-to-mouth resuscitation. Rashid and I knew she was dead almost as soon as we laid eyes on her, and we don't have medical training. Ned should've known it, too. Could he have messed with the body when he was doing CPR?" I slowed to seventy-five to hug a particularly tight curve in the road. Tires screeched. "I mean, there'd have to be a damned good reason to put your mouth on a cold corpse that had bugs crawling on it."

"Pull over!" Beth commanded.

I did. It was necessary. I apologized, tempered my driving, and avoided the topic of insect-ridden corpses.

We'd passed the Very Large Array satellite dishes and were approaching Socorro when I turned down the volume on a Paul Simon track and sought Beth's opinion again. "Did you buy Lyle's whole drama of curling up in a fetal position when he heard about Kendra? It seemed a bit over the top to me."

"There's something emotionally immature about him; he seemed more dependent on Kendra than most guys are on their wives."

"So the whole lying in a fetal position thing rang true to you?"

"Tess, almost nothing out there 'rang true.' Everything that happened seemed surreal—the visual effects of the sunset, the lightning storm, Kendra's death. It was like we were beta-testers for a new Universal Studios experience."

When we reached Socorro, priority one was to locate a rest room. We spotted the prominent adobe courthouse near the plaza. Lavatories and district attorneys couldn't be far off. I pulled into the parking lot.

Above the courthouse entrance someone had hand-painted the Seal of Socorro. The eagle within the seal appeared a bit deformed, as though one talon had a mild case of polio. I found the off-kilter raptor rather endearing; since my breast surgery, I'm a little lopsided myself.

The courthouse double doors opened onto a long hallway. I looked left and Beth looked right as we cased the joint for bathrooms. Treasurer's Office. Finance. County Recorder. Tax Assessor. At the end of the corridor, we spotted the Women's Room. As soon as we were done using the facilities (which were remarkable only for an overdose of tutti-frutti room deodorizer), I retrieved the business card Sheriff Garcia had given us and noted the address. The office was in an adjacent building right around the corner.

Beth was hungry, thirsty, and tired. If she'd been a twelve-stepper, she might be knee deep in cocaine, cognac, or caca by now. I volunteered for the first interview, gave Beth the car keys, and urged her to get something to eat. The receptionist, hard at work coloring in Lotto picks with a No. 2 pencil, ushered me in for an interview.

Can it be that I've so absorbed the sexism of my culture that I just assumed the DA's investigator out here in cowboy country would be a man? Perhaps. I hadn't really paid attention to the name on the business card, only the address. Now I was sitting in front of Chief Investigator Armida Franklin, a casually attractive Latina somewhere in her forties. Her medium length black hair was pulled back in a pony tail. She wore a yellow sundress, shiny bracelets, DKNY eyeglasses, and a wedding ring.

Her office was furnished with a metal desk, file cabinets and table, all putty gray. A framed photo of JFK delivering his inaugural address hung on one wall; on another was an award from the governor citing her accomplishments. Ivy, spider plants, and philodendrons intertwined among the stacks of manila files throughout the room. On her desk a framed snapshot of an Anglo male, whom I assumed was her husband, winked at her. A crinkled pink satin garter clung to one side of the picture frame. This was not the office of a typical bureaucrat.

The statement I'd given to Sheriff Garcia had apparently been faxed or emailed prior to my arrival. The Chief Investigator carefully reviewed it with me, then concluded with, "Hmmm. OK. Anything else?"

"Anything else?" That was it? How did she expect to get any real information with that technique? Wasn't she going to grill me? "Well, I would like to share a few things." I told her about my friendship with Sergeant Kari Dixon of the San Diego Police Department, and how I'd assisted in two murder investigations. I told her of my marriage to Roark—close association with a man who worked for a national security org couldn't hurt my image with law enforcement. I provided phone numbers and references.

Armida listened quietly. Finally she leaned back in her chair. A spider plant's chartreuse tentacles brushed the back of her head. She sat forward again, pushed her glasses down along the bridge of her nose, and drilled me a gaze. "You're not under any particular suspicion, Ms. Camillo. Why try to impress me with your creds?"

Her frankness disarmed me. "You know about the stun gun?"

She nodded. "So far it's the only possible murder weapon we've found."

"Oh, come on—'murder weapon'? Tasers aren't made to kill; that's the whole reason to buy one instead of a real gun, so you don't cause any real damage."

"True. But they can still be lethal, depending on how they're used, and the health of the person they're used on."

Damn. She had a point. "Well, the stun gun belongs to my friend Beth. She's in trouble and I *know* she's innocent. The reason I gave you all that info is, the more you know about me, the more you'll trust my ability to judge character. At least I hope it works that way."

Armida Franklin flipped through the as-yet skimpy case file. "Your friend is pregnant; I can see how you'd want to be protective."

"Beth's OB GYN has warned against too much stress. This baby means a lot to her, so please, if there's anything you can do to clear her quickly, I'd really appreciate it."

"Why was she carrying the Taser? Someone threaten her?"

"No; I think the pregnancy hormones have made her, well . . . let's say she's had exaggerated responses to things."

Armida laughed. "My hormones went *loco* during my second pregnancy. I get it. You have children?"

I shook my head no. "I lead a barren lifestyle," I jested over the hidden meaning.

There was a long pause almost as pregnant as Beth. Finally, "Who do *you* think killed Kendra?"

Flattered that she sought my opinion, I was about to expound when suddenly a new "Duh!" dawned. To obtain information, investigators can either intimidate suspects or they can win their trust. Armida Franklin, a non-athletic five-foot-three woman, had brilliantly mastered the latter technique. I'd known her perhaps fifteen minutes and I wanted to tell her everything I knew; everything I suspected. But should I? I watched her play with the bracelets on her arm, then shifted my gaze to the citation on the wall. This was an intelligent, diligent professional. And Beth and I had nothing to hide.

I shared some of my observations and doubts. "Rashid was anxious to be alone with Kendra's body when we first discovered her. He wanted Ned and me to go back to the cabin without him. He's probably nice enough, but that did seem weird. Of course, he wasn't the only one acting strange out there." I told her how Ned had administered CPR when it was blatantly useless. Finally I opined, "But if it is a murder, I guess I'd look most carefully at Lyle. After all, he was the only one who knew Kendra before we all got to the Lightning Field. Who else would have a motive? Spouses often make good suspects from what I hear."

"Did Kendra and Lyle seem to get along?"

"Yes; they seemed quite close." I thought over the events

at the Lightning Field, then added, "There was this kind of odd tension when we were talking about camping experiences. Kendra seemed intent on embarrassing him, by telling how friends made him pee his sleeping bag when he was a kid. I definitely got the feeling she had the upper hand in their relationship."

"Interesting," Armida commented as she scribbled notes. "And only you, Beth Butler, Rashid Prince, Ned Merkur, and the Theismans—were there at the Lightning Field?"

"Well, an employee of the Dia Art Foundation, Jorge, dropped us off. Come to think of it, he returned twice, too."

She leaned forward with interest.

I realized Sheriff Garcia had asked us to start our statements with what we were doing at the time of the lightning storm, the presumed time of Kendra's death. He'd never asked about earlier events. "When we arrived at the Lightning Field, there was nothing cold to drink so we asked Jorge to make a beer run. He came back with the beer, then Ned sent him out again to get some Scotch. He returned a second time, then left. But Kendra was alive and well when all that was going on."

Armida made notes. "Anything else?"

I thought for a moment. "A ranger stopped by to warn us about mountain lions in the area."

"That's odd. Do you remember his name?"

"I think it was George Calvin. No, Calvert."

Her eyes sparked with recognition. "Oh, I wondered why a ranger would go out of his way, but George is like that. He and his wife lost their only child many years ago; he's been parenting the whole world ever since. George is definitely one of the good guys."

"Well, Beth is one of the good 'guys,' too. I know you can't just cross her off your suspect list, but I hope you'll at least give her the benefit of the doubt. I don't know how Kendra died, but I promise you this: I'll do everything I can to help your investigation. Everything I learn, I'll share with you."

Armida nodded. "Good. People might tell you things they won't tell a law enforcement official."

It was almost 4:30 p.m. My stomach, for which this morning's breakfast was a Paleozoic memory, gurgled loud enough for Armida to hear. I thought the conversation might continue, but the Chief Investigator suddenly stood up, smoothed a wrinkle in her sundress, and offered a handshake. "Thanks for coming, Tess. Please send Beth in now if she's available."

In the lobby Beth swallowed the last bite of her veggie burger. She handed me a fast-food bag and a Coke, and went in to talk to Armida. The chicken nuggets and fries wouldn't do much for my waistline, but I scarfed them down like they were eats from Emeril.

Armida spent only five minutes with Beth. We both took that as a good omen and were soon completing the last leg of our journey back to Albuquerque. Aware that we were "persons of interest" in a legal investigation, and in consideration of Beth's anxiety about my driving, I practically crawled up I-25. It may have been my longest stretch of within-the-speed-limit driving since I first got my permit. I dropped Beth off at her house, carried her bags in, and hugged her good-bye.

As I unlocked the door of my extended-stay suite and walked inside, dual blasts hit me: welcome air conditioning and a not-so-welcome case of the blues. What is it about walking into an empty motel room that does that?

I unpacked my bag, tossed dirty laundry in a pile on the floor, cracked ice cubes loose from the small freezer's tray, and slid them into a glass. Found my bottle of Bombay Sapphire and poured.

I had a pale sapphire glow by the time I picked up the phone and called Lana. She chattered about French lavender, Finnish travel companions, solstice astrology, Pookie's ear mites, and her fiancé Gable. I told her about the Lightning Field. The exchange grounded me in what I needed: San Diego, the house, the dogs, and our deep contrapuntal bond.

When I got off the phone, I booted my laptop and checked my email. A response to my PlanetOut personal ad awaited.

> From: fem_reb@PlanetOut.com
> To: SanDiegoTess@PlanetOut.com
> . . . "Life Is Beautiful" and "The American President" hooked me. . . . what are the odds that my all-time favorite movies would end up on someone else's favorites list? I'd love to get to know you and talk more!
> Naomi
> P.S.—I did not have to look up "osculation" :)

Fem_reb. Hmmm. Femme rebel? She included a link to her profile. I scanned the personal information she offered. She billed herself as the executive director of a non-profit. Sounded harmless. She lived in the L.A. area. Not my backyard, but closer than Guam. There were overlaps in our favorite books, movies, and activities. The posted photo showed a woman about my age with wispy silver hair, clear green eyes, sculpted cheekbones, and a winning politician's smile. It was drool at first sight.

12

HI, HO, JUAN TABO

HI, HO, JUAN TABO; oh, he's the guy for me!

You have to hone your reflexes with espresso in order to navigate Albuquerque's Juan Tabo Boulevard without incident. As I headed downtown from the city outskirts where Bryce Corporation kneels at the foot of the Sandia Mountains, right lanes disappeared without warning. Left lanes were clogged with panicked drivers hastily deciding to turn. Detours and obstacles abounded. The Silver Bullet and I revel in this kind of driving. I wasn't sure who Juan Tabo was; in fact, no one seemed to know much about the fellow who lent his name to streets, taverns, public libraries, pets, and at least a few fake IDs. Nevertheless, I could tell he was my kind of guy.

When I first suggested to Beth that I should use extended lunch hours at Bryce to probe into Kendra's death, she balked. She sought nothing more than a return to normal. But two days after we left the Lightning Field, I got a call from Armida that indicated "normal" was a long way off.

"Tess," the DA Investigator began, "I checked your bona

fides with the San Diego police and others. You have people who'll really go to the ropes for you."

I silently thanked Roark and Kari, as well as *Our Gang* producer Harold Roach, patron saint of rascals everywhere.

"Even though you were at the Lightning Field, I've essentially eliminated you as a suspect. I'm choosing to view you as an ally in this case. This conversation is confidential. You understand what I'm saying?"

I assured her I did.

"Good. " She rustled some papers, requisite behavior for law enforcement types during phone calls. "The preliminary autopsy report confirms that Kendra Theisman's death was a homicide. Someone held an electrical device directly against her chest in the area of her heart, shocking her repeatedly until . . . " she began quoting from the report, " . . . the electrical current induced severe fibrillation resulting in myocardial infarction."

"They zapped her until she had a heart attack?" I verified.

"Yes."

"They're sure? There was a scorch mark on the ground where we found her, just like the other places where lightning struck. There's no way that . . . ?"

" 'Fraid not. A number of things weren't consistent with a lightning strike. The medical investigator said a lightning strike powerful enough to kill someone usually ruptures eardrums and Kendra's eardrums were intact. He also said there was no arborization—"

"Lightning can strike where there aren't any trees."

" . . . in a Lichtenberg figure. It's a term for the branching pattern of capillary ruptures typical of a lightning strike. The bottom line, Tess, is that the people who get paid to know this stuff were pretty sure."

I knew; deep down, I knew. I just didn't want to accept.

Armida continued, "Time of death was between three and three-thirty in the morning. According to the National Weather Service, the storm hit the Lightning Field around two-fifteen and lasted till about two-fifty. Kendra was killed after the storm passed." Armida paused again.

"Anything else?"

"The only fingerprints found on the stun gun were Beth's."

S-h-t and three-quarters. "How about the cauterization instrument Ned Merkur had with him? Could that have inflicted the wounds?"

"The medical investigator ran tests with it, but the wounds didn't match up. The cauterization pen generates heat, not current. Kendra's burns were secondary; what killed her were the repeated electrical shocks to the heart muscle. The medical investigator was positive that the cauterization pen could not have been the murder weapon."

"Did they have any ideas about what could have caused her injuries?"

"A stun gun or an electric cattle prod, something like that."

At least the pancake turners were in the clear. "Beth didn't do this, Armida. There had to be another weapon out at the Lightning Field that was overlooked."

Armida was one step ahead of me. "I've sent a team out to the Lightning Field. They're looking all around the cabin for disturbed soil where a weapon might have been buried. We don't have the resources to search the entire Lightning Field, but they're using a metal detector to check around the cabin.

The Catron County Sheriff's deputy said they already checked the well and tack shed, but I told my people to double-check them, just to be sure. The dry well was capped; they'll look to see if the seal's been tampered with. I don't think something as big as a cattle prod could be overlooked, Tess, but another stun gun is a possibility. If you've got suggestions, I'm listening."

"A wooden walkway—a kind of porch—runs around most of the cabin. I don't think the deputy looked underneath it when he searched the premises."

"We'll check it out. Can't hurt."

After I conveyed to Beth the gist of my conversation with Armida, she backed my lunch time snooping.

Spurred by moral decency, indecent curiosity, occupation, or obligation, a few days later, several dozen people attended Kendra's funeral at Albuquerque's Mt. Calvary Cemetery; Armida, Beth, and I were among them. Lyle moved through the service like a sleepwalker. His father, a down-to-earth widower who ran a local bakery, stayed close by him. Kendra's parents had flown in from St. Louis, along with her twenty-two-year-old sister, Caitlin. Her parents were about my age; the father, a divorce lawyer; the mother sat on the board of the St. Louis Historical Landmarks Association. Caitlin was about to begin a master's program in architecture. Though their expensive haircuts and quality clothing said things about them, their obvious shock and grief spoke even more loudly.

Coworkers from the university art department also paid their respects, but it was the presence of three tearful Down's Syndrome students from Kendra's volunteer work that affected me the most. They mourned Kendra's loss with an emotional honesty that shamed the rest of us.

Although Lyle was the most obvious murder suspect, his mental state seemed genuine. But "seemed" can be slippery. I needed to investigate. Knowing that Lyle would be occupied with the awful business of death for at least a few more days, I decided to nose around his bicycle shop. After the service I headed on down Juan Tabo Boulevard.

Lyle's business was on Central Avenue near UNM, not far from Saggio's Pizza. When I was in the vicinity, I parked the Silver Bullet at a fast food joint and walked from there, to avoid the tyranny of the parking meter.

The address on Lyle's business card matched a stucco building that squatted on the corner of Central and Tufts. I opened the front door on Central and walked into a neighborhood barber shop. A few old gents looked up from their *Albuquerque Journals* and off-track betting sheets. Nary a bike in sight. I tipped an imaginary hat to them and departed. Apparently the building housed more than one business. I tried again and found the real entrance to Lyle's bike shop around the corner on Tufts, not Central. Why don't these things ever happen to Joe Leaphorn or Kay Scarpetta?

This time when I opened the shop door, smells of oil, grease and rubber, not shaving cream and hair tonic, hit me. To my right was a service counter separating customers from display racks of bike accessories, with a small repair bench where a lone employee concentrated on a gear box. The wall behind the repair area hosted rows of tires and inner tubes.

Aisles of new bikes filled the floor space to my left. I wandered around, inspecting rubber tread and price stickers. Lyle sold kids' bikes for $60, fancy mountain bikes for $2,600, and everything in between. One racing bike was spangled in tawny gold with red flecks. The sales tag called the color Dirt Fire Green. I'd have to think about that one.

I was drawn to an end cap display featuring a 144-spoke Lowrider wheel. The play of sunlight on all those spokes mesmerized me. If you stared hard enough, a parabola arose from the center of the wheel. Hallucinations without drugs. Impressive.

"Need help with somethin'?" A scratchy smoker's voice disrupted my enjoyment of the optical illusion.

I turned to see the youth who'd been working on the gear box. His mustache and frame were as scrawny as his vocal persona was scratchy. *Gerald* was sewn on the pocket of his overalls.

"I'm here to see Lyle. Is he available?"

"Uh, no. His wife just died. He took the week off for the funeral and stuff."

"That's terrible. What was it, a car accident?"

"No, she got hit by lightning out near Quemado."

"Jeez, no wonder he forgot our appointment." OK, better quit acting before the ghost of Lee Strasberg haunts me. Time to see what I could learn. "I'll reschedule with Lyle, but maybe in the meantime, you could help. I'm a business consultant. Lyle hired me to help him maximize profits for the store."

Gerald gave me a blank look. Maybe the fact that I'd offered no name and no business card inhibited his response. At least I'd thought to bring a notepad and pen. I persisted. "What's the most profitable item in the store?"

"Uh, that'd be these." He pointed to racks of mirrors, seats, and horns near the cash register. "Accessories got the biggest margin."

He knew what a margin was; he was brighter than he looked. I pretended to make notes. "OK, that helps. And what's the best selling item in the shop?"

That one stumped him. I tried again. "Does anything sell so well that you have trouble keeping the item in stock?"

"Yeah. The Sweet Pea."

This time he stumped me. He explained, "Dahon's lightweight portable bike. Folds up not much bigger than a laptop."

He handed me a brochure illustrating a cute-as-the-dickens baby blue bike that folded to 11″ × 22.5″ × 27″. "That's adorable! I want one!"

"That's what everybody says. Got six or seven backlogged orders."

I made more notes. Lyle had access to tools in the repair shop. What if he had somehow managed to hide an electrical tool in the cabin somewhere? "Would you mind very much if I went back there for a look?"

Reluctantly, Gerald allowed me through the gate behind the counter and into the repair work area. I spotted pliers, cables, wire cutters, wrenches, calipers, gauges, and a small acetylene welding torch but nothing that looked lethally electrical in nature.

A customer entered the store with a young boy in tow. Gerald eyed them for a moment, then turned back to me. "You better come back Monday when Lyle returns."

"When Lyle and I talked, he seemed devoted to his wife. But, of course, since you work for him, you know the inside scoop." My inflection made it a question.

"His wife was pretty hot for an older chick."

If Kendra in her late twenties was "an older chick," I suppose I passed for mummified. I nodded, encouraging Gerald to share whatever scuttlebutt he might know.

"Lyle's a nice enough guy, but kinda average. Know what I mean?"

I nodded again.

"This tore him up real bad, that's what I think."

Yes, losing the woman you love can mess you up worse than tequila with a worm or a Camaro without brakes, a truth to which I gave little thought as I engaged in that evening's email exchange.

From: SanDiegoTess@PlanetOut.com
To: fem_reb@PlanetOut.com
Your profile says you're the director of a non-profit. What kind of non-profit?
Tess

From: fem_reb@PlanetOut.com
To: SanDiegoTess@PlanetOut.com
I work for an organization that gathers genetic information on Jews and Arabs to trace common ancestry, in an effort to establish a bond between Israelis and Palestinians (and all of the other Middle Easterners from which Jews are essentially alienated). And hold onto your hat. Or rather, your yarmulke: I'm a rabbi. Ordained even. That's what the "reb" in fem_reb stands for—rebbe.—
Rabbi Naomi Roth

From: SanDiegoTess@PlanetOut.com
To: fem_reb@PlanetOut.com
Naomi,
Is it true you people have a Burning Bush? Hope so.
Tess

13

PINKEYE

THE TROUBLE WITH A ROSY worldview is that it may be due to pinkeye. I knew I wore rose-colored glasses when it came to Ned; I just plain liked the guy. Yet reason dictated that either he, Lyle, or Rashid had murdered Kendra. I decided to nose into all-things-Ned, and to hope that what I learned would allow me to eliminate him as a suspect. I told Beth I needed Monday off, and early Saturday morning I aimed the Silver Bullet toward Vegas.

Between Albuquerque and Gallup on I-40 the landscape resembled wheat toast with dabs of penicillin mold. I zoomed past a "Trust Jesus" sign nailed to a cottonwood. Cattle ranches stretched across the horizon offering only flies and moos to punctuate the emptiness. I cruised past the teepees where Native Americans, in an exquisite role reversal of the original Manhattan land purchase, offer pricey trinkets to tourists. As I drove through the town of Winslow, a line from an Eagles song came to mind, something about a girl being such a fine sight to see.

The fine sight I wanted to see wasn't in Winslow; she was probably stuck in traffic on an L.A. freeway. Her name was Naomi and I was already looking forward to her next email.

We all have dirty little secrets. What's yours?

OK, I'll go first. Mine is that for all the Rabelaisian romps and satyric boinking I've indulged in, I still seek the brass ring—true love. I believe it'll be there if only I reach far enough, am patient enough, wise enough, sensitive enough, and maintain a distinguishable waist line.

I spent my youth getting the lay of the land, so to speak. By my thirties, I'd done a hitch in the Navy, earned my master's, and enjoyed close encounters with many women. There were women who liked to spell the word "womyn" and leave "men" out of it entirely, apparently unaware that "y" is the male chromosomal determinant. There were women who liked to be called dykes and women who hated to be called dykes. There were women who'd never slept with men and at least one woman who denied ever sleeping with women, even as I returned her thong which had slipped beneath my pillowcase the night before.

I made mistakes; did the U-Haul thing a few more times than I should have, but was always able to extract myself essentially intact. And then at a party where I blew out thirty-nine candles on a Key lime pie, I met Lana. The hostess introduced her as the best massage therapist in San Diego. Lana *did* know how to touch—physically and emotionally—ah, but there's the rub.

Now that I'm closer to fifty than forty and savvy enough to know my brass from a Kegel ring, I sometimes wonder if the prize has eluded me. Did my true love lie in bed with me one night and I failed to recognize her? Would I know the timbre of her voice or the rhythm of her walk?

I stopped for a burger and coffee in Flagstaff, and tried unsuccessfully to halt the internal monologue that kept looping back to the romantic potential I sensed in Rabbi Naomi Roth. Oddly enough, some of the appeal was her vocation. My father's family are ex-Roman Catholics who long ago veered off into fundamentalist nether regions, but my mother was a nonpracticing Jew. Naomi dedicated her life to a spiritual tradition that, at least on some level, resonated in my very marrow.

There was also a titillating forbidden fruit aspect to dating a clergy member. I'd never done it before; had never given it a thought. But now that the possibility loomed, I found it strangely enticing. And it wasn't just her job that drew me: if her online photo was even half accurate, she was a stone cold fox.

Of course, things might change when we met. The real person behind her profile might be a thirteen-year-old boy in Wyoming who wet the bed. She might have wicked halitosis. She might leave toenail clippings on the carpet.

But I wouldn't bet on it.

Betting was best reserved for blackjack tables and video poker machines in America's Paradise Lost. Miles and miles rolled by until the horny neon of Vegas finally flashed into view.

Before I left Albuquerque, I'd found addresses for Ned's house and his Off the Map Museum in an online directory. I entered his home address in my car's navigation system. Following the directions, I turned off Desert Inn Road, drove through a neighborhood so ordinary it would bore vanilla, and arrived in the 3600 block of Cielito Lindo Avenue. I cruised past Ned's house, circled the block to get my bearings, and parked a few doors down from his place. Ned's home was a seventies stucco with two desert willows out front to provide shade for the scrubby canker of a front lawn. The maroon Xterra he'd driven to Quemado rested silent in his driveway. I grabbed a Fuji apple and chunk of cheddar I'd brought with me, got out and stretched. It was about eleven at night; no one else was around.

I bit into the apple as I walked. It felt marvelous to move and stretch after so many hours in the car. The streetlights were barely adequate; if I was quiet, I wouldn't attract attention.

I cautiously walked up the drive and peeked into Ned's SUV. A blinking red light on the dash indicated a security alarm was activated. Ix-nay on the idea of riffling through the glove box. I crouched down and slunk to the rear of the property. Two lights were on inside the house, one where I thought the kitchen might be; the other, probably his bedroom. I couldn't do much prowling if he was awake. But even though I was road-weary, I wanted to accomplish something before settling in for the night.

Three trash cans stood behind his house near the garage. I lifted the lid off the first and was treated to a waft of suppurating garbage. The second was a recycling can for bottles and other glass items. Judging by its contents, Ned bent the elbow more than occasionally. The third held a payoff of sorts: stacks of shredded business papers. How hard could it be to fit those strips of paper back together? I scooped up an armful and crept back to my car.

I backtracked to the Strip and took a room at the Flamingo. I'm not sure why I find its Pepto Bismol décor comforting, but I often stay there when I'm in Vegas. I dumped the shredded paperwork into the plastic bag designated for hotel guests' dry cleaning. I was too tired to deal with that today. I took a hot shower, the perfect antidote to garbage snooping. The hotel room got Showtime and I allowed myself an *L-Word* rerun as a bit of foreplay. Finally, when I could no longer resist the temptation, I opened my laptop and checked my email.

From: fem_reb@PlanetOut.com
To: SanDiegoTess@PlanetOut.com
I'm off to Grosse Pointe for a fundraiser tomorrow. Airport security, here I come.

More than delightful to hear from you. Take care . . . and keep in touch!
Naomi

From: SanDiegoTess@PlanetOut.com
To: fem_reb@PlanetOut.com
I drove from Albuquerque to Las Vegas today. Long road hours gave me a better appreciation for why people fly in spite of airport hassles. An acquaintance of mine lives here. He's intrigued by cattle mutilations and government conspiracies. Tomorrow I'll visit his Off the Map Museum, to learn what the Feds are hiding in Area 51. If I'm not back for supper, Gracie, it may be that I've *become* supper . . . somewhere on Betelgeuse.
Tess

14

OFF THE MAP

THE NEVADA TOURISM BUREAU calls it the Extraterrestrial Highway. I thought I'd be cruising State Road 375, but when I punched the address of Ned's museum into my GPS system, the directions sent me past taco joints, taverns, and mobile home parks decked in dust and gravel, past scruffy palms and deep into the northeast corner of Las Vegas. Electric cables, telephone poles, water towers, and loud billboards chopped the view of raffia-colored mountains to the east. The sky reflected a stark sterile blue, perfect contrast to the aesthetic seduction of nights illumined by the Bellagio fountain.

I found Ned Merkur's Off the Map Museum directly across from the "I" Street gate of Nellis Air Force Base. Nothing like getting right up in the face of the powers that be. Or the powers that bomb.

I paid an admissions clerk $2.75 and entered the modern one-story white stucco building. Inside the museum's cool darkness, I expected doe-eyed alien kitsch. Instead, three walls were covered with breathtaking full-color enhanced satellite maps of Area 51, revealing topographical details of Groom Lake and its surroundings. Most of the museum's visitors were clustered near these maps. The map walls also displayed legal briefs, letters, and other documents, some from the Air Force, in which long segments of text had been blacked out.

In the center of the main room, a round table featured plastic 3-D models of complex molecules. No alien intestines, no crashed capsules from space ships. What kind of Area 51 museum was this?

Dramatic portraits of Hitler, Joseph McCarthy, and General Pinochet hung on the fourth wall. I wandered in that direction. Between two portraits of Hitler, signs warned citizens not to give their government unconstrained power, but rather to make government answerable to the people. Text panels between the portraits expounded on what happened when citizens were not vigilant, explaining how all three men had abused their power. Along the same wall hung news photos of gassed Kurdish tribesmen and the victims of the 1995 Tokyo subway Sarin attack.

While interesting in a libertarian sort of way, I didn't understand how it all fit with Area 51. Disappointed, I turned away from the display, and found myself literally face to face with Ned Merkur. In gray Dockers, striped shirt, and tie, he looked less like a leprechaun and more like a middle manager. His skin seemed flushed and sweaty even in the museum's air conditioning. He blinked hard. "Tess?"

Since my face was only inches from his, I decided the question was rhetorical. I stepped back and shook his hand. "Ned!

Some friends of mine came with me to Vegas this weekend for a little R & R; we're staying at the Flamingo." Better not to let a suspect know I was traveling alone. "You and I never got the chance to talk about your theory of what's out in Area 51. So I figured as long as I'm here, I'd come visit your museum." I was babbling, but ironically this seemed to relieve Ned. He flashed a grin.

"Well, welcome! Come on over here and look at these babies." Ned gestured toward the molecular models.

I read the captions: ricin, diacetoxyscirpenol, *botulinum, Clostridium perfringens,* T-2, and other biotoxins.

"I built these myself. I wasn't able to identify all of their components, but I came pretty close." Suddenly Ned took my arm and rather forcefully led me down a corridor off the main museum room into his private office. My antennae alerted, but relaxed when he left the office door open.

Strewn across an oak desk were his vet's bag, a taxidermied porcupine, remnants of Chinese take-out, a rolled up poster, tubes of modeling glue, various newspapers and magazines, a bottle of ketchup, a John Mayer CD, file folders, two empty brown beer bottles, unopened mail, a birdhouse, and candy canes still in their wrappers. The rest of the office made the desk seem organized.

He moved a piece of electronics gear from a chair to the floor, offered me the now-available seat, then sank his own butt into a swivel chair behind the desk. "Sorry about whisking you in here; I didn't want the tourists to follow us. This is my sanctuary." He sniffed the Chinese take-out and tossed it into a waste basket. "Did you see Diane Sawyer's feature about

Area 51 on *60 Minutes*? It would've been, oh, a decade ago at least."

"Not that I remember." I glanced at the electronics piece he'd moved to the floor. An old stereo receiver maybe?

"Then I'd better start at the beginning." He fiddled with a paper clip. "Like I told you out at the Lightning Field, I used to be a vet. Back in the eighties I worked with the FBI on a special project investigating cattle mutilations. Based on that experience, I concluded that the federal government was excising organ tissue samples from livestock, for reasons unknown. The fact that the FBI didn't know what was going on meant the CIA or the Pentagon was behind it. Which was entirely credible—you wouldn't believe how many reports there were of black helicopters in the vicinity of the mutilations." He pulled a folder from a drawer, located a map of the U.S. and spread it across his desk. "Here's Area 51," he said, pointing to a sector on the map. "Here's where most of the livestock mutilations occurred." He indicated a trail of blue dots that ran throughout southern Utah and Colorado and northern Arizona and New Mexico. Notice anything?"

"They're all reasonably close to Area 51; closer than Delaware, anyway," I ventured.

"Exactly. I believe there's runoff from the groundwater at Area 51 to all of these locations." He put the map back in the folder and looked at me. "I think the U. S. military deliberately and illegally disposed of biological and chemical weapons in Area 51—weapons we weren't supposed to have, mind you. Then the Pentagon needed to know how far those toxins may have contaminated the groundwater. They couldn't just go up to families in Durango or Santa Fe and say, 'Hey, can we biopsy your kid's liver?' So they took random samples from the organs of livestock to do their analysis."

"Is that what Diane Sawyer concluded?"

"Sawyer interviewed Jonathan Turley, an attorney who represented past and present employees of Area 51 in a class action lawsuit. They claimed they'd been forced to dispose of biochemical weapons in unsafe ways. One of the men Turley represented, a guy by the name of Robert Frost, died from complications due to exposure to biochemical toxins. His autopsy showed an unusually high level of dioxins in his system. But *60 Minutes* never tied Area 51 in with cattle mutilations."

I nudged the electronics box with my toe. A police scanner, maybe. Looked like one. "So that's what all the secrecy is about at Area 51? Bioweapons?"

"I think that's what it *was* about. I'm pretty sure they're not doing it any more."

"Then why continue to keep everything so hush-hush?"

"The Air Force still uses Area 51 to test experimental aircraft; that was always one of its purposes. But now it's mostly a diversion. The public bought into all the alien crap; it keeps people focused on Area 51, where there's really not much going on. I doubt there are any alien spacecraft or corpses on earth, but if they do exist, the Feds would stash them somewhere else—some place you don't hear about on lurid TV specials."

The good-natured humor I associated with Ned was gone. Although controlled, he seemed deeply angry. I thought about what he'd said, especially the mention of children with liver toxicity. I looked around the office for family pictures, but didn't see any. "Did the government do something to your family, Ned?"

His shoulders tensed, just for a heartbeat or two. Was that a soupçon of panic? Or was I imagining things?

"What family, Tess?" he asked. "I have two married sisters in Illinois and a senile father in a nursing home. I've been divorced thirteen years; I'm not even sure where my ex-wife lives. Sacramento, I think."

"Children?"

"One that lived; a daughter. Rachel. Her mother has had custody since . . . well, Rachel probably wouldn't know me now if she fell over me." He sighed. "I own responsibility for some of it, Tess, but you're right—I do blame the government for harming my family. But not with biotoxins." He unwrapped a stale candy cane, broke off a piece and sucked on it. "I didn't lose interest in being a veterinarian. I lost my license." He seemed to sag into his chair a bit. "After my work with Project BOVMUT, the powers that be decided I was too vocal about my suspicions concerning biochemical weapons. The U.S. wasn't even supposed to have them; it was against several international treaties. Suddenly I found myself faced with numerous professional complaints and malpractice suits, all of them lies or gross exaggerations. But it got too expensive to defend myself. Eventually, my veterinary license was revoked. I couldn't support my family. There were other stressors on the marriage, but . . . "

"Maybe you could talk to that attorney, Jonathan Turley?"

"He's too busy to take me on. He's been involved in lawsuits about all kinds of nefarious deeds our government has perpetuated, especially concerning FISA." Ned shook his head. "No, long ago I came to terms with losing my license. In fact, I have more freedom now that I don't need the government's permission for my daily living." His glance swept out toward the museum. Some of the twinkle returned to his eyes. "The Off the Map Museum is my revenge."

I looked out the office window at the harsh heat of the day. My gaze moved across the street to the base entrance. "I love the moxie of putting this right across the street from Nellis Air Force Base. Do you make a reasonable living?"

He studied me for a moment, deciding something. "This museum is—quite intentionally—the biggest legal tax shelter I'll ever manage." He smiled. "Tax breaks shouldn't only be for the rich, right? I mean, the big players use all kinds of loopholes. Great-West Lifeco saved five hundred and fifty million in taxes with a slick trick called the 338(h)(10) election. Five hundred and fifty million—get your head around that! And it's legal. My little tax rebellion is on a much smaller scale. Nevertheless, it gives me satisfaction."

"I'm beginning to understand."

"Right in their front yard, I'm thumbing my nose at their secrecy by displaying maps of Area 51—accurate, detailed maps. And I'm making sure no more dollars of mine fund any more biochemical weapons . Or cattle mutilations. My tax returns show losses, year after year."

"You've found a way to cope with personal loss and do something purposeful, by educating the public."

He stood up. "I'm hungry. Let's grab lunch."

We left together. This time he didn't have to drag me down the hall.

15

GILA GUTS

THE GILA GUTS SALOON, across the parking lot from the museum, looked pretty much like you'd expect from the name —dark, lean, full of testosterone, with better heads on the brews than on some of the customers. The saloon didn't serve food, but was a willing conduit for Mexican specials from the eatery next door. Hazy smoke drifted through the saloon, at least some of it from a cheap cigar. Johnny Cash rumbled a cowboy aria in the background. "Nice place, Ned. Very upscale."

"Let's talk about what's really on your mind: murder." His candor caught me off guard and the glint in his eye told me he delighted in that. "We both know that a murder barely a week ago is a lot more intriguing than old rumors about Area 51, especially since we were right there when it happened." He slid a Mexican food menu across the table toward me. "Their tamales are good."

My eyes were still adjusting to the dim light and smoke when a young Goth took our order. I asked for a Corona, hoping Ned would order tongue-loosening booze, too. Instead, he ordered a Coke.

We fumbled through small talk about the sadness of Kendra's death until the Goth deposited beverages and two heaping plates on our table. As soon as she moved away, Ned declared, "It had to be Lyle."

The tamales were perfect. "You don't think Rashid could have slipped out in the middle of the night to do the deed?"

Ned swallowed a bite of his fajitas and considered. "He could have; I can't say it's impossible. But he would've had to be really quiet about it. I'm not sure how it was in that room where you and Beth slept, but in the main house we heard every footstep, every flush. If Rashid was up in the middle of the night murdering Kendra, I think I would have heard something."

"Yeah, we seemed to hear every little squeak in our part of the cabin, too."

Ned fidgeted with the coaster under his Coke. "I think Rashid's a spook."

I had to process for a few seconds before I realized he wasn't using the racist epithet of the fifties but the rather spy term of the sixties. "Why? Did he leave a secret decoder ring on the night stand?"

Ned shrugged. "Just a feeling I've got. He's Middle Eastern. His father was a military officer. And the CIA is always recruiting people who understand that culture, right?"

I gave a noncommittal shrug. Ned was capable of seeing black helicopters and Big Brother even in the few places the Patriot Act hadn't let them penetrate. "Did Rashid talk about anything in particular? You must have had some conversations."

"He mentioned his young son Ramo several times, and if I remember right, he said his wife was an optician. He said that sketching relaxed him. I saw his sketches—he didn't have much talent. Basically he was alert and quiet." Ned added, "He did a lot of observing, just like a spook."

"Rashid did buddy up to Sheriff Garcia, didn't he?" I remembered. "He was the first to volunteer to be searched."

"I peg him for Homeland Security, although what Homeland Security would be doing out at The Lightning Field, I don't know. Anyway, if Rashid's a spook, and if you and Beth aren't Lizzie Bordens, that leaves Lyle. It's logical. He's the only one who knew Kendra before we got to the Lightning Field, right?"

"That was my thinking; I told the DA's investigator as much." I savored my last tamale bite. "But if Lyle's a murderer, he had me fooled. He and Kendra seemed so happy together."

The Goth refilled our drinks with a pout and left the check. "I'm not sure Lyle is psychologically sound," Ned offered. He watched longingly as I swigged my Corona. "Lyle seemed like an odd duck, kind of emotionally immature. Know what I mean?"

I nodded. "Maybe he had a breakdown of some sort."

Over at the bar, a potato-skinned rancher fumbling his way through an 80-proof fog knocked over his Seven & Seven and demanded a free replacement from the bartender.

Ned laid money on the table to cover our check.

"Thanks; I'll leave the tip." I stood up and contributed a few bucks to the Goth's studded future.

When we walked out of the Gila Guts, glaring sun stung my eyes. Once again, blinded by the light.

On the drive back to Albuquerque, I'd been rolling along

the asphalt leviathan for four hours when Armida phoned to ask if I'd learned anything relevant about Ned. "He's paranoid about the federal government, probably with good reason. Thinks the military dumped biochemical weapons in Area 51. He's got an ex-wife and a daughter; claims he's not in touch with either one." I paused to pass a monstrous motor home, then continued, "Two things—Kendra's father is a divorce lawyer. I think Ned's own divorce was tough on him. Ned went to the University of Illinois and Kendra's family is in St. Louis. I don't know where he was living at the time of the divorce, but it would be interesting to see if Kendra's father handled Ned's divorce." I turned down the volume on the car radio so I could hear better. "And my other question is, could Kendra have been Ned's daughter? From what I can gather, Kendra and his daughter Rachel would be pretty close in age. You might want to verify his daughter's whereabouts, just in case."

"Kendra's parents were at the funeral, Tess. They were either her real parents or the best actors I've seen since Oscar night."

Good point. "She could be adopted. Anyway, I just suggest it as a 'dotting all i's and crossing all t's' measure. To be honest, Ned does seem like a decent sort. He cares about people's safety and health; otherwise, why would biotoxins in Area 51 energize him so much? I don't really see him murdering Kendra, but I figure it wouldn't hurt to check up on his daughter."

"I appreciate your feedback, Tess. Thanks." Armida was definitely one of the more gracious law enforcement types I'd ever met. "Do you remember Dale?"

"The Lightning Field guide; the one Jorge substituted for?"

"Right. Dale returned yesterday from his trip. When we questioned him, he thought he remembered seeing an electric cattle prod stored in the old tack shed behind the cabin at the Lightning Field. He's not certain, but at least it's a possible murder weapon besides your friend's Taser."

"Did you find a cattle prod anywhere around the Lightning Field?"

"Not yet, but we haven't given up. The dry well had been capped for some time and the seal was still in tact, so no one ditched any kind of weapon down the well. I've got people searching roof rafters, the porch walkway, and of course, the tack shed. If there's a cattle prod in the area, Tess, we'll find it."

A second phone call came later in the evening. Beth's voice burbled with the rapture of a flamingo in Fantasia. "Tess, the most marvelous thing just happened!"

"Well, don't keep me in suspense."

"I was lying back, soaking in my bathtub, relaxing. Suddenly I felt this fluttery, squiggly sensation in my belly. I looked down and I saw—I *saw*—the baby move!"

"Hot damn!" I shared in her Juno-esque elation until I spotted a highway patrol car and moderated my joy back to seventy miles per hour. "Don't worry, Beth. We're going to find out who murdered Kendra and clear you of suspicion. You need to focus all your energy on becoming a mama."

Criminitlies, now she had me talking like a turkey baster baby booster! I entertained myself the rest of the trip by making up song lyrics that included "turkey baster baby booster," "rubber baby buggy bumpers," and "Gila Guts Saloon." Weird Al Yankovich would've been proud.

16

SOCIAL ENGINEERING

I GREETED MY BLARING alarm clock with the same level of enthusiasm the Tin Man reserves for Brillo. I'd gotten back into Albuquerque only six hours earlier. Half asleep, I showered and brewed a pot of Sumatran Mandehling.

On my agenda was not a database at Bryce (Beth had given me the day off) but rather what computer types sometimes refer to as "social engineering." Others might use a more quaint term—flimflam. I needed to look like a middle-aged, non-threatening, and completely forgettable woman. Given that today's temps would probably reach 105 degrees, I slipped into white jeans and a sleeveless red and white dotted Swiss top. Vanilla with a few daubs of cherry. Perfect.

When the java had jostled me awake, I dialed Lyle's father's bakery, knowing that any bakery worth its yeast is open early.

"Adore Your Buns Bakery," a chipper voice answered.

"Hi, I'm conducting a survey on behalf of Mega-Swirl Electric Mixers. Can you answer, oh, maybe thirty questions for me?"

"Uh, let me get the owner. Hang on."

I quickly hung up. Task number one—determining the father's whereabouts—successfully completed.

After another cup of coffee, I phoned Lyle's bike shop. The shop assistant, Gerald, told me that Lyle wasn't in yet, but he was due back at work today and was expected any minute. I now knew Lyle was on his way to work, and Lyle's father—the only family member who lived locally and might be staying with him temporarily—was at the bakery. Lyle and Kendra's home should be at my private disposal for snooping.

Around 9:30 a.m. I picked up a small ham and a quart of potato salad at a local deli. At a thrift store I found a pan for the ham and a bowl for the potato salad. My plan would work better if the food looked homemade.

According to the phone book, the Theismans lived in Albuquerque's Victory Hills neighborhood, south of the UNM campus near the Islamic Center of New Mexico. I found the address easily, a single story, henna-colored adobe apartment building with blue trim. The only access to the building appeared to be through the wrought iron gate in front.

I parked on the street, placed the food carefully inside a brown paper bag, and carried the bag with me to the gated entrance. As I expected, the gate was locked. Inside, I could see a courtyard which contained a few potted palms, a soda machine and two patio tables with chairs. I found Lyle's name in the list of residents. I buzzed his apartment and received a satisfying silence. Then I pressed the button labeled "Building Manager."

A husky female voice with an East European accent answered. "No solicitors how can I help you?"

Time for that social engineering. "Hi!" I tried to sound as cheerful as if I'd actually gotten a good night's sleep. "I'm a friend of Lyle Theisman—the tenant who just lost his wife? I've brought him a home-cooked meal. He didn't answer his buzzer. I guess he's back at work already. Could you let me in his apartment so I can put these things in his fridge?"

"I come out there wait."

She was as good as her word and much better than her punctuation. I soon stood eyeball to St. Stephen's medallion with a six-foot-tall woman in a red apron who introduced herself as Janka Szili. "I manage building can't let you into apartment but if you want I can take food and give it to Lyle when he come home."

A nice offer. A decent woman. The sun bore down on us. The ham was emanating a rich clove scent. Janka sniffed. I gave her one of those direct looks that politicians use when they're about to call a tax hike an investment in the future. "You know, I should probably water his plants, too. Lyle can walk right by an ivy that's shriveling from thirst and . . . "

An enormous crack, like a big tree limb snapping, ruptured the conversation. I ducked as Janka flinched. The noise came from the first apartment on the right. Before I could catch my breath, Janka shoved open the gate, grabbed a set of keys from her apron pocket and ordered, "Come with me now we go!"

Maybe thirty seconds later, Janka unlocked what turned out to be the Theisman's front door and we walked into the living room. In moccasins, blue jeans and a yellow golf shirt, Lyle sat in a La-Z-Boy chair. Eyes closed, his luxurious dark eyelashes caressed his cheeks. They were too beautiful for a man, especially a man with a .22 pistol in his lap and a bullet hole on the right side of his head.

"Na!" Janka yelled. Dealing with suicidal tenants was decidedly not in the fine print of her contract.

I tossed the decoy meal to the floor and checked Lyle's neck for a pulse. "He's alive!" I called 911 and gave a surrealistically calm report. Janka was churning s's and z's into a string of Hungarian exclamations. "Can you go out front and watch for the ambulance?" I asked her. "You'll need to let them in the front gate."

Janka pulled her sizable self together and departed.

I bent over Lyle, lightly touching his shoulder. There was surprisingly little blood. It looked like he'd held the gun a foot or so away from the right side of his head and fired through the very front of his brain. Swallowing your gun—blowing out the back of your head and brain stem—is arguably the most surefire suicide method. Since Lyle's wound was far from the brain's control centers for breathing or heart beat, maybe he would survive.

"Lyle," I whispered. "Can you hear me?" I saw his eyes move slightly under the lids, and a muted sound escaped his lips. "An ambulance is on the way," I reassured. "Hang on, kid. Hang on." For the briefest moment, I wondered if I was offering encouragement to a man who had murdered his own wife. His suicide attempt could be prompted as easily by guilt as remorse.

As though he read my mind, he mumbled, "Needed her too much." Then he lost consciousness.

As I waited for help to arrive, I desperately wanted to

snoop. I wanted to inspect every drawer, cabinet, and closet; search for journals, letters—anything that might yield clues to Kendra's murder. But I also realized any fingerprints or trace evidence I left behind would compromise the scene, and no one needed that.

I scanned the immediate area for a suicide note. Nothing. My eyes did a broader sweep of the living room. A large distinctive art print in reds and blues hung above the plain crimson sofa. Since Kendra taught printmaking, it was probably one of her originals. The older maple coffee table held a newspaper, bicycle magazines, and toenail clippers. A small stand held an ordinary TV and DVD player. Window curtains closed. The room smelled of gun powder. No suicide notes; none out in the open anyway.

Lyle groaned. Mouth-to-mouth resuscitation isn't the right fix for someone with a bullet in the brain who's still breathing. And you can't put a tourniquet around someone's neck to keep the head from bleeding. So I uttered inane, generic reassurances to the unconscious man. "You're going to pull through, Lyle. Hang on, hang on, hang on."

A team of police and EMTs blew through the door and went to work. The cops quickly secured the scene, ascertaining that Lyle and I posed no threat to others. Then the EMTs did a speedy assessment. One placed a clear plastic breathing mask over Lyle's face. Another grabbed a large IV needle. I suddenly felt nauseous.

I'm a needle-phobic. I can't watch an addict shoot up on TV without feeling like snails are eating my spleen, so I decided this was the perfect moment to do a walk-through of the place while everyone was busy or distracted.

I touched nothing.

The kitchen was decorated in yellows and orange with a whimsical fruit motif. A loaf of bread, a jar of peanut butter and two unopened bills lay on the kitchen counter. No back door from the kitchen.

The dining room, just big enough to hold the simple oak table and chairs, held no surprises other than expensive silver candlesticks. A wedding gift?

I walked past the bathroom with its overflowing laundry hamper, and entered the bedroom. The drapes were drawn. Large windows, but no back door here either. I caught the faint whiff of incense. Lyle's guitar case leaned against the wall in one corner. A pair of jeans lay on the floor. A black and beige comforter had been hastily pulled up over rumpled sheets. Lacquered black bookcases held fantasy, sci-fi, art books, and biographies. Between books I found the incense burner, along with framed family photos. A second shelving unit held a stereo and CDs. Kendra and Lyle's wedding portrait hung on the wall over the bed. Here and there, tiny bird's nests and polished glass stones added color and texture to the room, more signs of Kendra's artistic influence, I guessed. All in all, the place looked normal; homey, even, if you didn't go in the living room.

I went to the living room. Lyle's head, loosely covered with gauze, had been secured between two blocks on a spine board, which was now being carefully bound to a gurney. The words he had whispered haunted me: "Needed her too much." Had he resented how much he needed his wife? Was that a confession? Or was that a justification for why he'd put a bullet in his own head; an admission that he couldn't function without her? Whatever it meant, I was sure Armida would agree it had implications for the investigation into Kendra's murder.

I phoned Armida and left her a voice mail message. I'd just snapped my cell phone shut when a police sergeant approached to take my statement.

17

TESSELLATION

THE LOOK AND SMELL and sense of violence saturated that afternoon: Janka's panic, the acrid scent of gunpowder, those thick lashes, the baking heat, fragments of skull poking through the wound. But sitting across from me now was the look and smell and sense of promise: Beth's radiant skin, her fervent emotions, the fetus' life-force, like a phoenix rising. These opposing sensibilities dovetailed like the birds and fish in an Escher tessellation. Was death flapping dark wings or was life swimming upstream?

After I gave my statement, several calls to and from Armida had proven necessary before the Albuquerque police would let me go. Let's just say that being an out-of-state lesbian who appeared at the scene of two acts of violence in less than two weeks didn't endear me to them. Fortunately Armida interceded in time for me to meet Beth for dinner. We were dying to compare notes, although in light of police suspicions, clearly I needed to find a new metaphor.

Beth had suggested the Olympian Café in the Nob Hill

neighborhood. Wafts of oregano, garlic, lemon, spearmint, cumin, and paprika seduced me as soon as I stepped inside, and found that Beth had arrived just before me. We ordered at a busy counter and went to wait at a table in the back of the dining area. I sat facing the front of the restaurant where broad windows allowed a view of passers-by.

Beth took a call on her cell. It was Garrick at Bryce with an after-hours problem. While she put the corporate fire out, I watched the flow of tourists, *chicas,* students, homeless, gurus, and Gen X couples doing the sidewalk shuffle. Not so long ago, had Kendra and Lyle strolled by this same restaurant holding hands and laughing?

Our order came up. I retrieved Beth's eggplant dolmas and my spanakopita, both accompanied by generous sides of Greek salad and buttery pita bread.

I hadn't eaten anything since I'd left my efficiency motel that morning. God knows where the ham and potato salad were by now. The fresh-flavored food offered here soothed my nerves, and Beth ate heartily, too, like she was, well, eating for two. When we'd taken the edge off our hunger, we got down to business.

Beth slipped her cell phone back in her purse. "So what do you think? Did Lyle try to kill himself? Or does someone want both of the Theismans dead?"

"If someone shot Lyle and dropped the gun in his lap, that person was a real Houdini. Janka and I didn't see anyone leave as we were going in, and the front door of the apartment was the only way out." I took another bite of pita. "In the few seconds it took Janka and me to react, it's possible someone fled

Lyle's apartment, hid in the courtyard behind the soda machine, and escaped when we went inside."

"Sounds far-fetched," Beth remarked as she rolled a Greek olive around in her mouth.

"It is far-fetched. But so is a perfectly pleasant young woman dying in the middle of the Lightning Field from multiple electric shocks to her heart. There's some weird shit coming down, if you haven't noticed."

"Point taken. Did Lyle seem remorseful to you? You were right there; you must have formed an impression."

"My impression is that people's motives are hard to read when a bullet takes the A-train through their forebrain." I knew Beth would breathe easier if Lyle was guilty of his wife's murder, which would clear *her* of all suspicion. I wanted to offer that comfort. But I really didn't know whether Lyle had shot himself from remorse or loneliness. If, indeed, he *had* shot himself.

Beth targeted another olive from the remains of her salad and popped it into her mouth. "Umm, I never realized how good these are!" A long sip of peach Snapple followed. "OK, let's say Lyle's innocent, that he tried to commit suicide because he missed Kendra so much. From what you've told me, your trip to Vegas left you believing that Ned is innocent, too. That means Rashid must've killed Kendra, right?"

"I think I should check him out very carefully." I blotted my mouth with my napkin. "You had some conversations with him out at the Lightning Field. Did he mention where he lives?"

"No, only that he worked as an insurance investigator. But

he gave me his business card." Beth searched for the card in her billfold, and got all teary-eyed and hormonal when she couldn't find it. She finally located the card in a zippered purse compartment and passed it to me.

The card declared that Rashid Prince was a Fraud Specialist III at the Alliance Security Insurance Company in downtown Los Angeles. "He's from L.A.," I observed. "No wonder his son doesn't know much about camping or fishing. When I get back to San Diego next week, I'll pay him a visit; see what I can find out." I pulled out my compact and checked my teeth for strands of spanakopita spinach. All clear. "Ned thinks Rashid is with Homeland Security doing some kind of intelligence work."

Beth looked skeptical. "Do *you* think he's a spy?"

"Whether he is or isn't, he still could be our murderer. Working for Homeland Security doesn't make him a Girl Scout; quite the contrary."

"I need more olives," Beth announced with an intensity that alarmed me. I bee-lined it to the order counter to see if I could procure additional supplies.

I was returning to our table with a bowl filled with the slippery orbs when I glanced out the windows and saw Jorge Mantilla, our AWOL Lightning Field guide! I was almost positive it was him, wearing blue jeans, a red tee shirt, and a black kerchief, just like the one he'd worn at the Lightning Field. I plopped the bowl in front of Beth and handed her a few bills from my wallet, while explaining my sudden departure. She had no time to object.

I ran out the front door, scanning the area where I'd spotted him. He was gone. He had been approaching a side street when I'd seen him. I ran down the main drag, University Avenue, then jogged into that side street. I saw the back of a man wearing a red tee shirt. He was too far away for me to catch up with him on foot, so I returned for my car. By the time I traced that side street, he had disappeared and so had most daylight.

I wound my way along one block after another, driving slowly, scrutinizing groups of men huddled together in the evening air, smoking and laughing. I noticed fewer street lights in this part of town, and occasionally garbage festered along the sidewalk. I turned down another street and thought I spotted him. The light was so dim that I couldn't be certain the shirt was red, but it sure looked like Jorge. The car windows were up for the A/C, but I rolled my driver's side window down and shouted, "Jorge! It's Tess. From the Lightning Field. Can we talk?"

The man turned, looked at me, then increased his movement in the opposite direction. I rolled my window back up and tried to follow. After five more minutes of dark streets, I was rapidly losing any optimism about this pursuit. I second-guessed myself about whether it had even been Jorge that I sighted. If it was, it was pretty clear he didn't want to join me for tea and crumpets.

At the next stop sign, ominous shadows enveloped me. The Silver Bullet and I suddenly were surrounded by youths who were definitely not selling *Readers Digest* subscriptions. As two of them blocked my way, several others pushed and rocked my car. One bad ass screamed profanities at me and swung a tire iron into my passenger door window, shattering it. Criminitlies! I lived long enough in Jersey to know how to deal with this shit. I revved the Silver Bullet's engine, blasted the horn and took my foot off the brake. One body dove to the left; another to the right. Only when I'd reached the end of the next block did I remember to exhale.

I'd seen a bullet in someone's head before noon, had been emotionally tessellated at dinner and had just incurred serious repair costs for the Silver Bullet. I needed the comfort only a rabbi could offer.

18

ON THE ROAD AGAIN

WHILE I WAS CONCERNED for Beth and challenged by the question of who killed Kendra, some dormant part of me was experiencing a little kick, a boost in spirits. *Be still, my heart. Stand up, my clit. Roll over, Beethoven!* My connection with Naomi rekindled hope for a romantic bond and stoked the possibility of an end to months of self-imposed chastity. I felt a flush in my veins and a bounce in my step that I'd been missing.

From: SanDiegoTess@PlanetOut.com
To: fem_reb@PlanetOut.com
This is NOT live from New York on Saturday night. :) This is road-weary from Holbrook, Arizona (between Gallup and Flagstaff) on Friday. I needed a break from driving so I took the Holbrook exit, and parked near the town courthouse. Booted my laptop, and discovered they actually have a wireless signal out here. Imagine! Now if only they could do something about shade when it's 108 degrees. The glare makes the laptop screen hard to see; forgive typos.

A meteor fell on Holbrook in 1912, and the town bills itself as the Gateqay to the Petrified Forest, so there's a sense of both the dangerous and the dead. Which brings me to the topic of my recent escapades—something I need to share with you out of fairness before our acquaintanceship goes any further. Rather than email, let'd talk. 619-555-2833 (cell). And when we do email, you don't have to go through PlanetOut. My personal email is: freepi4all@gmail.com. That's "pi" as in the ratio of a circle's circumference to its diameter. I majored in Math. After I majored in History. A little like "I voted for it before I voted against it."

You probably have Shabbat services Friday evenings; can we talk tomorrow? Call me.

I'll be staying among the red rocks of Sedona tonight. As for now, it's back to spreading my glory along Route 40.
Tess

The next morning anxiety, excitement, and dread took turns cluster-stompin' me as I waited for my cell phone to ring. I had a hard time paying attention to traffic. When Naomi hadn't called by noon, I began the second-guessing game—the one where we try to guess another person's motives or reactions, while having no facts to base our opinion on. I was desperately afraid that I'd freaked out the lovely rabbi with my allusion to danger, death, and "recent escapades." Why would she want to get involved with someone who had such fearsome cautions to divulge?

I missed an exit. I nearly ran out of gas. I spilled my coffee. Where were the gentle cottonwoods, stark mesas or exit signs for Montezuma's Castle between Sedona and Phoenix? I had no idea. My eyes were open, but my vision was clouded by anxiety. Why had I emailed such a weird message? Why did I feel compelled to divulge my involvement in murders and maybe a suicide? Why didn't I just let things develop slowly, naturally? Damn, I love women but hate this dating stuff.

I was peeing at a Denny's where I'd stopped for soup and salad when the phone finally rang. An L.A. area code; I knew it was her. Should I answer it now, and let her hear a flush in the background? Flush first, then answer?

From: freepi4all@gmail.com
To: fem_reb@pccoalition.org
Good to talk to you today. Thanks for understanding my desire to help find Kendra's killer. When we talked about my friend Beth's pregnancy, I was surprised to learn that you're a mom, too. How old is your daughter Eileen now? My mother's name is Eileen; your father was born in Atlantic City, three miles from my hometown. Is our destiny written in the stars? :)

You asked if I had to describe myself in terms of TV show characters, who would I be? Thought about that tonight as I cruised toward Yuma. Do you remember the Golden Girls? Well, I have the mind of Dorothy, the libido of Blanche, and (though I don't like to admit it) the soft-heartedness of Rose. Which, by the way, is far better than having the mind of Rose, the libido of Dorothy and the soft-heartedness of Blanche—all of which will make no sense unless you know the show. My housemate Lana reminds me of Rose—they both travel through life on a slightly different wavelength from everyone else around them. I once had a conversation with Lana about the relative merits of degrees, referring to my Bachelor's and Master's. I later learned that Lana thought we were talking about Fahrenheit and Celsius.

Let me turn it around: which TV show/characters do you relate to most? Hope it's not Pushing Daisies: I'm highly tactile.

Staying at the Yuma Cabana Motel tonight. Up early tomorrow for the three-hour zip in to San Diego. I'll be back in time for the big sandcastle tournament next weekend. Nothing like a little sand in my shorts to make me feel at home.
Tess

From: fem_reb@pccoalition.org
To: freepi4all@gmail.com
I enjoyed our phone conversation too, though I prefer email. I spend so much time on the phone at work that I get tired of it. Glad to hear you and Lana have remained close. My ex, Joanne, and I are friends, too. My daughter Sharon Eileen (who now insists on going by her middle name—a form of teenage rebellion if you ask me) turns seventeen in September.

Tomorrow I leave LAX for Philly at the hideous hour of 6:15 a.m.. Back in So. Cal next week. Hope we can meet shortly thereafter.

I most relate to C.J. Cregg (Allison Janney) on West Wing, though I'm only 5′7″. And yes, I know the Golden Girls. I find your Dorothy/Blanche balance a most appealing combination!
Naomi

Interesting. I'd never thought of C.J. Cregg as the least bit rabbinical. Toby Ziegler, maybe. But C.J.? Naomi was full of surprises. I opened more emails.

From: A.Franklin7thDist@da.state.nm.us
To: freepi4all@gmail.com
Tess, Getting back to you about the whereabouts of Ned's daughter Rachel. We located Rachel, 17, and her mother, Connie, in Stockton, CA, where Rachel attends Lincoln High School. She lives with her mother, who has resumed her maiden name of Ashburne. And just to be certain, I verified that Kendra was not adopted. Also, the lawyer who handled Ned's divorce was Elliott Bradshaw of Moline, Illinois. Don't feel bad—both leads were worth a try. Let me know if you have other ideas.
Regards, Armida Franklin

From: freepi4all@gmail.com
To: A.Franklin7thDist@da.state.nm.us
Re: Jorge
More loose ends tied up, but meanwhile, another has arisen. Just before I left Albuquerque, I thought I spotted Jorge walking on Central Avenue one evening. I tried to talk with him, but if it was Jorge, he wasn't interested in connecting. Just thought you should know.
Tess

From: Beth_Butler14@bryceinc.com
To: freepi4all@gmail.com
Hey, friend—Everyone at Bryce misses you; Jeanette, Garrick and Dano all say Hi. Lyle's hanging in there. Doctors say he'll have some brain damage but not as much as you'd think, considering. He confirmed to the police that this was a suicide attempt. But when they asked if he shot himself out of guilt because he killed his wife, he just stared into space. Guess that answer will have to wait till a shrink gets him to open up. I'm anxious to know what you find out about Rashid. Be careful!
Beth
P.S.—I sent your final Bryce paycheck to your San Diego address
P.P.S.—I've started to pick out baby names!

These last messages were exchanged at home. My home: the Missions Hills neighborhood of San Diego, where you breathe a bit of Pacific mist with every inhalation; where donut vendors do not package weasels and where the Chargers may break our hearts in the fourth quarter. Home: where Raj's licks, Lana's hugs and a paycheck awaited. Where I fell asleep in my own bed, snuggled against a pillow I once danced with.

19

SUSPECTS IN THE SAND

SCRATCH BENEATH MY FIRST eight layers and you'll find a Jersey shore beach brat. By the time I reached kindergarten, I could judge how high the tide would rise by the location of mussels on pier pilings. I knew that horseshoe crabs had bright blue blood. I could recognize the rasp and skitter underfoot that meant I'd stepped on a sting ray.

When I was four, my favorite way to spend a summer afternoon was to romp in the bottle green ocean for hours until I was tired or thirsty. I'd reluctantly emerge from the water, run to where Ma sat under her beach umbrella (scarf around her hair, modest bathing suit discouraging flirtation) and ask for a soda. She'd tell me she knew I'd stayed in the water too long because my lips were purple and she'd dab my nose with Coppertone: that was almost a ritual between the two of us. I'd drink a Coke, retrieve my plastic bucket, and go dig in the sand for mole crabs.

The vernacular for the odd little crustacean *Emerita talpoida* was "sand flea" but what did I care about that at age four? The sand was rife with these speedy creatures that didn't bite or pinch. They looked like miniature VW Beetles cloaked in gray plastic. Only an inch or two long, they seemed perfectly constructed by the universe as live entertainment for my age group. I'd build a sandcastle with crenellated walls and drizzled spires, and relocate a few mole crabs to luxurious new castle digs.

Forty-five years later, the joys of the Imperial Beach Sandcastle Contest had nothing to do with urban renewal for mole crabs. This weekend, amateur and professional (yes, professional) sand sculptors would compete for over twenty-thousand dollars in prizes. If only I'd known I was on such a rewarding career track at the age of four, I could've skipped college.

Lana joined me for my excursion to the sandcastle contest. The day was typical San Diego: blue sky paradise with temps around eighty degrees—Fahrenheit, not Masters. Children scampered about; the sun spangled the Pacific. Bands hired by the contest sponsors played at high volume, which at least had the advantage of drowning out the squawks of seagulls. Beach umbrellas and orange trash barrels splashed vibrant color on the serene silver gray beach palette.

Lana was in a downright loquacious mood, sharing with me seven new uses for lavender and anecdotes of her sojourn in France. We hadn't had much time together since I returned. She spent most of her free time with Gable; it didn't require a major leap of imagination to realize she would soon give notice and move in with him. Which, I suppose, was as it should be. We'd been walking and talking companionably for half an hour when finally we reached the area where dragons, elves, castles, and other manifestations of sand crystals, white glue, and imagination stretched as far as we could see.

We spread our blanket in the spectator zone beyond the yellow plastic strips that barricaded the sandcastle projects. To our left was a massive octopus sculpture, with a tentacled circumference the size of Rhode Island. To our right, three teens decorated a sand Buddha with Celtic runes. Too many multicultural workshops?

I'd been trying to solicit Lana's opinion on the Lightning Field murder, but it was hard to explain the cabin layout as we walked. Once we settled on our blanket, I did what I'd so often done in childhood: I used the sand. Running my finger through the silver granules, I drew a diagram of the cabin. "That night Kendra and Lyle slept in this front room; Rashid and Ned took the room near the bath. And Beth and I slept over here. See?"

Lana scratched a fly bite and studied my sketch. The small scar on her upper lip, sustained when we confronted a megalomaniacal killer several months ago, hadn't tanned like the rest of her face. Seeing it gave me a pang.

I burrowed my toes into the sand. "It pretty much has to be Rashid, right?"

Lana pointed to my drawing and indicated the road leading to the cabin. "Could someone else have driven out to the Lightning Field in the middle of the night?"

"We would have heard a car or truck."

"During the lightning storm?"

I squinted into the sun and thought about it. The storm had been noisy with thunder booms and lightning cracks and rain pellets pounding the cabin roof. "OK; it's possible."

"So you could consider the ranger and Jorge suspects, too?"

"Why not just suspect everyone with a vehicle within a hundred-mile radius of the Lightning Field?" I snipped.

"Did everyone within a hundred-mile radius know Kendra was there?"

She had a point. Kendra's murder did seem personal; the victim, intentional. If I ruled out a random killing by a wandering homicidal maniac, then the murderer had to be someone who knew Kendra was there with us. Which added only Jorge and the ranger as suspects. Could the ranger or Jorge have doubled back to the cabin in the middle of the night? Had there been fresh vehicle tracks in the mud that morning? No one had noticed. And when the sheriff and medical investigator arrived, their vehicles would have destroyed any earlier tracks.

The Catron County sheriff had issued an APB on Jorge, and the ranger should be easy enough to track down if we needed him. For now, Rashid remained at the top of my suspect list.

The sun's warmth felt good. I reached for a bottle of water from our cooler. I failed to grip it properly and it rolled onto the blanket. "Sorry," I muttered.

Lana reached over and took my left hand. She ran her fingertip over the raw scar in the middle of the palm—my personal talisman of our encounter with the man who mutilated and murdered a rock musician. "Whatever you decide about this Lightning Field thing, Tess, be careful. Your curiosity has consequences." She said it without rancor about her scarred lip; she said it without pity about the hole in my hand. But she said it with an emotional veracity that only Lana knows how to convey.

20

ANTICIPATION

CARLY SIMON'S "ANTICIPATION" would be the perfect anthem for those nine days that passed between my return to San Diego and the day I met Naomi—nine days filled with cyber-courtship and a few breathy phone calls. I would soon need a housemate; who knew how things with Naomi would evolve? Everything good, everything sweet, seemed not only possible but waiting just around the corner.

> From: fem_reb@pccoalition.org
> To: freepi4all@gmail.com
> The summer sidewalks of Philly are slick with gray rain, but I am one happy rabbi! Whatever else may come from this bond we're forming, finding an intelligent, witty, educated, sexy woman to connect with has definitely boosted my optimism. I feel more attractive and more willing to risk than I have in years. Right now I'm jammed, putting together a special collaboration with the Genographic Project for an upcoming conference. When my schedule calms down and we can finally meet . . . how about Laguna Beach?

If we met for dinner somewhere, I already knew what we'd want for dessert. How would we keep our hands off of each other in public? But offering to rent a motel room on a first date with a clergy member seemed presumptuous, to put it mildly—burning bush or no burning bush. And you can't find a decent motel room in Laguna Beach this time of the year without a reservation. How should I handle this?

From: freepi4all@gmail.com
To: fem_reb@pccoalition.org
Laguna it shall be—not too long a drive for either of us and neutral turf. Do you like Italian food? We could meet for dinner at Ti Amo Ristorante on South Coast Highway. The eats and atmosphere are amazing, but it's pricey. An alternative scenario: a picnic on the beach, complete with a loaf of Italian bread, a bottle of good Valpolicella, and lasagna we heated up in the microwave of (do I dare say it?) our motel room. :)

From: fem_reb@pccoalition.org
To: freepi4all@gmail.com
Your alternative scenario bears a remarkable similarity to one I've rather shamelessly envisioned. Though I'm gearing up for a big conference, I may be able to clear my calendar on Thursday. I don't have anything booked then that I wouldn't gladly reschedule on our behalf! I would have to head back the next day by noon, but I'll happily take whatever time we can get sooner rather than later. Can you make that fit your schedule?
Naomi

An amusing question. I had no job or contract at the moment. My daily routine consisted of sleeping in, taking Raj and Pookie to Dog Beach, doing laundry, going to the gym, and indulging in bouts of online flirtation. Could I fit our first date into my schedule? Without even looking at a shoe horn!

In spite of our candid flirtation online, or perhaps because of it, when we'd talk on the phone, Naomi tended to focus the conversation on her work. She had few traditional rabbinical duties, although occasionally the havurah (Jewish congregational community) that sponsors her non-profit asks her to serve as a substitute rabbi if other clergy are on vacation or ill. While she is affiliated with the havurah, she spends most of her time educating people about her cause, attending meetings and raising money. Her conversations revealed Machiavellian strengths and a taste for organizational politics.

From: freepi4all@gmail.com
To: fem_reb@pccoalition.org
You seem to me to be a very complex woman—part of you is strong as hell, politically savvy, hard-nosed, strategic. Part of you (I think, hope, intuit) yearns to not have to be strong every moment, to not have to be wary of undercurrents, hidden agendas, and power structures; wants simply to yield. Sure hope I'm right about this second part, because I'll sound like an idiot if I'm off the mark. But whether I'm right or wrong, your evident complexity will make getting to know you quite intriguing.

From: fem_reb@pccoalition.org
To: freepi4all@gmail.com
Tess, darling, you're freaking me out (just a little) ! How can someone I've known for such a short time, and only from a distance, so comprehend my heart's deepest yearnings for room to make my mark in the world, yet the freedom to just "be" at home? And why don't you seem threatened (as others have been) by the energy and passion I have for my work? Yet you promise

plenty of passion of another variety in a way that makes my knees tremble and gives me a continual secret smile.
Naomi

From: A.Franklin7thDist@da.state.nm.us
To: freepi4all@gmail.com
RE: Jorge Mantilla
The man who called himself Jorge Mantilla was an undocumented worker using a false ID. From fingerprints we managed to identify him as Francisco Gutierrez of Ciudad Juarez. He has a criminal record in Mexico for check forgery. Friends we interviewed said he came across the border to get a fresh start. Because he's involved in a murder investigation, I suspect Mr. Gutierrez has returned to Mexico and that we won't be hearing from him any time soon. You probably saw someone who resembled him.
Armida

From: freepi4all@gmail.com
To: fem_reb@pccoalition.org
I found us the perfect place! The Cottage suite at the Casa Laguna—from its web site, it looks romantic and there's a sofa bed in the sitting room. If our chemistry doesn't work when we meet in person, I can sleep there. I don't want you to feel forced into anything. Let's meet at 2:30 p.m.. I'm bringing a special bottle of wine. You said you wanted to contribute the food—great; I appreciate that. I don't eat mayonnaise, bananas, or stinky cheese. Almost anything else works.

Thanks for the card you sent. I can't get over how a woman I've never met knows EXACTLY how to flirt with me, how far to go to absolutely tantalize, yet never go so far that it's unseemly. In all the emails and phone calls, your sensuality, sexuality, flirtation and teasing have been 110% perfect. How do you do that? I hope to find out soon!
Tess

From: fem_reb@pccoalition.org
To: freepi4all@gmail.com
I've been wondering the same thing myself—how do YOU get inside MY head and say precisely what I need to hear to feel safe to be my full sexual self with someone I haven't even met yet? How do you manage, with both sensitivity and sass, to seduce me so compellingly? You seem to offer precisely the yang my yin yearns for.
Naomi

From: freepi4all@gmail.com
To: fem_reb@pccoalition.org
In exactly 24 hours, I will see your face. If anything should happen between now and then (freeway accident, terrorist strike, who knows these days), know that you have made me very, very happy. Soon. . . .
Tess

Several favorite outfits, cleaned and pressed, hung in my bedroom closet. A new pair of earrings I'd bought just for the occasion lay on my jewelry box. On my dresser stood the wine I'd special ordered: RBJ's Theologicum, an Australian red that, by virtue of its name, seemed appropriate for a first date with a clergy member.

It was finally going to happen—woo hoo! Once again, life was full of meaning. The sky was bluer, toothpaste was mintier, I felt ten pounds lighter, even Raj's breath smelled better as he willingly received my exuberant, if displaced, affections. I danced my way down the hall from my bedroom into the living room where Lana was spending a rare evening at home watching CSI. She had never watched crime shows until recently. I think my sleuthing has had a bad influence on her.

Lana let me babble about my plans for Laguna. "In tomorrow's chart, the secondary rulers of the decanate and quadrant signs are the Moon and Venus. That bodes well," she offered cheerfully.

I understood that about as well as I understood Janka's Hungarian. When CSI was over, a Jerome's Furniture commercial came on, swiftly followed by a pitch for Oggi's Pizza. Lana said she was heading to bed. I wanted to switch channels. "Where's the remote?"

She lobbed the remote wand to my end of the sofa. "I see no barriers to this new perspective, Tess, all channels being equally accessible from the screen with a wave of the remote fish named Wanda."

I was still puzzling over this Lana-ism when I tuned into a VH-1 special on the hundred greatest love songs of all time. When they got to #56, "The First Time Ever I Saw Your Face," I felt a lump in my throat.

21

THROUGH THE LOOKING GLASS

THIS WAS NOT THE Holiday Inn on prom night.

Occupying the entire second floor of a building behind the pool, the Casa Laguna's Cottage Suite offered primo privacy and an unobstructed ocean view. The entryway opened into a sitting room with a massive Mission-style fireplace. French doors led to the bedroom where, beneath an open-beam ceiling, a king-sized bed awaited. Fresh calla lilies sipped from crystal stem vases on the night stands. The leaded window panes were trimmed with blue stained glass. A tasteful living room, kitchenette and bath completed the suite. Whitewashed rustic brick walls greeted the eye throughout, and everywhere I turned, the nuanced décor whispered of romance.

I arrived twenty minutes early so I'd have time to freshen up. I brushed my teeth twice and combed my hair for the fifth time. Straightened the collar of the black and white kokopelli shirt I'd picked up on my way through Sedona. With black jeans, it helped hide the weight I'd gained in New Mexico. The bathroom mirror reflected what I already felt: I looked damned good today.

I unpacked some of my things. Placed the Theologicum wine on the kitchen counter, put another bottle (a reliable white zin) in the fridge, and located a corkscrew and glasses. Turned on the bedroom ceiling fan so it wouldn't get stuffy in there. Put several CDs in the stereo. We'd never discussed music, so I'd brought a variety: Alicia Keys, Dar Williams, k. d. lang, Los Cafres, Coldplay, and Chopin. If all went well, one or more of those artists were going to create a whole new definition of sheet music.

When I'd done everything purposeful I could think of to burn off nervous energy, I stood at the top of the stairs and waited for Naomi.

Suddenly, there she was—a tropical garden of green and pink flowers crowned with silver. She was probably well aware of what her outfit's color did for her malachite eyes.

My face must've expressed my pleasure, because Naomi looked up at me from the stairs below and said, "Tess, you have a feral smile."

All I could muster was the fierce urgency of "Wow!"

She continued climbing the stairs, cool as Grace Kelly on the rocks with a sprig of spearmint.

I moved aside to let her enter and caught a whiff of something wholesome and clean. She put down her purse, an overnight case and a Trader Joe's grocery bag, and stood in front of the fireplace, her gaze simultaneously pulling me closer and keeping me at a distance.

If I'd first seen her somewhere in public without knowing

who she was, my initial impression of Naomi would've been that a popsicle wouldn't melt in her orifices. Most Jewish women I know project a warmth imbued by their culture, but Naomi seemed as effusive as mercury. Certain women are fueled by a heat hidden and unexpected, with geysers that erupt from within their own tundra. Did her frost hide fire? I had to know.

I leaned her against a wall, held her hands behind her back and pressed my lips against hers. We kissed and kissed, then kissed some more. The charge between us sparked an arc 180 degrees from the one that had struck Kendra Theisman. This one was life-giving, born of delight and passion, but every bit as potent. I definitely would not have to sleep on the sofa bed.

With smiles we could scarcely suppress, we chattered and fumbled about. I took her Trader Joe's bag into the kitchen while she settled her things in the bedroom and bath.

When she rejoined me, she noticed the Theologicum label on the wine bottle. "Delightful! Will you pour?" She found Gouda and rye crackers among the groceries she'd brought and arranged them on a platter. For a moment I felt like I was on a hot date with Martha Stewart.

I raised my glass. "L'chaim!"

"You have a good Hebrew accent. You sure you're not Jewish?"

"Actually, I am half Jewish. My mother's side. Which makes me Jewish enough to know that *bupkas* is not 'butt kiss' mispronounced."

We laughed nervously, taking each other's measure, our words whirling in subtext. The wine tasted spicy but subtle; we drank our first glass mighty fast.

I couldn't take my eyes off her. She was every bit as good looking as her online pictures had led me to believe, but what photos could not convey—what I was now experiencing for the first time—was her charisma. This was a woman who drew everyone's attention when she walked into a room; a woman who could and would accomplish things.

Conversation was nearly impossible. A month of emails, phone calls, hopes, and dreams, along with our in-person chemistry created a sexual tension that sucked the oxygen from the space between us. How long could we last?

I managed perhaps another thirty minutes, then reached out for her hand. "I want to make love with you. Are you ready?"

Immediately something shifted. The cool, self-possessed politician's persona evaporated. With what I can only call radical vulnerability, Naomi took my hand and followed me into the bedroom.

I excused myself and went to the bathroom. I returned wearing a black muscle shirt and a black leather contrivance Paladin would have envied.

Naomi lay naked between the sheets, searching my eyes for something, her manner soft and receptive. If she was an ice queen, this bed was not your father's Frigidaire.

I stood beside her. Her silver hair was mussed against the pillow. I pulled the top sheet down far enough to reveal her breasts and caught my breath.

"Gorgeous," was as verbal as I could get. I removed a calla lily from its vase and stroked its waxy white curl under her chin, then slowly, slowly, across her breasts and along the inside of her elbows.

"Ooh, ummm . . . "

I pulled the sheet all the way down. "My, my, my!" She was already glistening.

I climbed in beside her, burrowing my face in the damp valley between her breasts. Even in the summer afternoon heat, her skin smelled like baby powder and coconut with a hint of Calvin Klein One. Clean and inviting.

My mouth moved to her nipples where I marveled at their responsiveness. My thick fingers danced against her hidden cache, tapping and teasing.

I lowered myself on her body, spread her legs, and took a good long look. What I saw reminded me of my favorite iris—an exotic cultivar called "Wither Thou Goest." Sweet coincidence: the iris name comes from the Bible story of Ruth and Naomi. Like the flower, my Naomi offered frilled petals of pinkish lavender and mauve, with a burgundy sepal drawing the eye toward a center that promised glory.

I was too aroused to hold back any longer. I raised myself up again and slid inside her. She wrapped her arms around my neck and lifted her hips to meet me.

A primal growl escaped my throat. Oh god oh god oh god.

Yes, she was physically attractive to me. Yes, we'd imbibed several glasses of wine. Yes, I hadn't made love in a while. Yes, our anticipation had built up over a month. Yes, her out-of-bed cool pushed some button that dared me to melt her. Yes, yes, yes . . .

And yet. And yet. And yet. This was something more intense than I'd ever felt before. Touching Naomi produced nothing less than platinum sparks tingling down my spine. Entering her brought a sexual intoxication on a scale I didn't know existed; fifty kinds of neurotransmitters splashed my brain circuits. I was tripping on Naomi almost as powerfully as I had tripped on blotter acid at that '82 Talking Heads concert.

And it was mutual. Oh, yes: it was mutual. Naomi was not an experienced or knowledgeable lover, but she followed my lead with willing trust and sexual abandon even when we journeyed places she'd apparently never been.

Remember the first time you felt the summer grass between your toes? Remember the ecstasy? The sheer delight in wriggling your toes without shoes or socks, feeling the blades tickle? That was what I felt—that state of first grass or perhaps, first grace. Our every move came from a reservoir of unconstrained fervor we somehow enabled each other to tap into, and I trembled with the utter rightness of it all.

"Release yourself upon me," k. d. lang sang.

And Naomi did. She collapsed on me, nestled her head into my chest and sobbed. Had I died at that moment, I would have left this world a totally fulfilled human being.

Later I drove us down South Coast Highway to the oceanfront Heisler Park where we strolled for an hour, taking in scenery as breathtaking as any on the southern California coast. It was tourist season, so there wasn't anything you could call privacy, but we needed fresh air and space to clear the endorphin fog in our heads.

We passed by a public sculpture situated in a garden—an interestingly curved phallic shape set atop an orb. I walked over to it and caressed its girth. "Remind you of something?" I teased, then tried to kiss my new lover.

But Naomi pulled back, maintaining her aloof public persona. Maybe it was a clergy thing—no kissing in public? Ah, well.

After a while we realized we were hungry and zipped back to the Cottage Suite. We got comfy in our robes, and Naomi cooked us dinner. With efficient movements, she chopped chicken breasts, broccoli, red peppers, and onions, and stir-fried them with Thai noodles and olive oil. Her grin told me she enjoyed showing off her culinary skills.

I put the now-empty Theologicum bottle in a recycling bin behind the kitchen. I must've returned sooner than Naomi expected because I caught her sneaking a pill bottle from the grocery bag. She popped a pill, then returned the bottle to the bag.

Uh, oh.

I didn't let on that I'd seen her, but when she went to the bathroom a few minutes later, I checked the pill bottle and read its label.

When she returned, I opened the chilled white zinfandel and poured us both a glass. I lifted mine. "A toast!"

She raised her glass expectantly.

"In Beano, veritas!"

She blushed and laughed. "You caught me! I didn't want to take any chances with broccoli, you know . . . "

"Hey, I took one, too. Glad you brought them." I wondered how many people she could be this natural, this real, with.

We took our dinner and wine out to the living room. I parted the curtains that had been closed against the daytime heat. There in the purple twilight, we watched a scrimshaw moon float above the Pacific, silhouetting palm trees in the foreground. I put my arm around her waist; the moment became a prayer.

She offered a different kind of prayer in Hebrew for our meal. I was feeling rather grateful myself, for all kinds of sustenance.

Gradually the outside world disappeared for us. We cocooned in the living room and let the conversation drift, sharing stories about our parents, childhood, politics, favorite movies, good books, spiritual experiences.

After a while I asked, "Did you remember to bring the photos?"

She located several snapshots in her purse, and handed them to me. She stood next to my chair, pointing and giving me the 411.

"That's my daughter Sharon. Who now goes by Eileen."

"Well, Sharon Eileen is a looker, just like her mom," I observed. "Who's the guy with her? Your dad?"

"My ex-husband, Freddie. I was married for seventeen years." The tone of her voice went polar.

"Seventeen years; that's a long time. Were you in love with him?"

"I thought I was when we married, but what did I know? I was only twenty-three; he was forty-two. I'd gotten my degree in Global Studies at UC Santa Barbara, but wasn't sure what to do with it, so I took an admin job at Cottage Hospital while I figured it out." She paused. "Then along came Freddie. . . ." Naomi spilled her wine.

I scrambled for a towel from the kitchen and helped clean up.

"Let's see," I said, picking up where we left off, "I was asking what Freddie is like?" I was genuinely curious. Someone who spent that many years with her had certainly played a major role in her life.

"He's OK." No emotion; nada. She fixed her gaze on the wet spot left by the wine. "I hope this doesn't stain."

Her beige satin dressing gown looked new; I could see why she didn't want it ruined, but damn if I know how to remove a white zinfandel stain from satin. Naomi went looking for stain remover in the kitchen.

The whole spilled wine thing seemed to perturb her, so when she returned a few minutes later, I offered her a foot massage. That cheered her right up. I used a special almond oil I'd brought with me, part of Lana's professional masseuse supply.

I was sitting across from Naomi on a Victorian rattan chair, rubbing the oil into the arch of her right foot when she opened a new subject. "You mentioned you had breast cancer a while ago. What's that been like for you, Tess?"

How to explain? "I'm like the history of western civilization: Everything's divided into B.C. and A.D.—before cancer and after the diagnosis. At one point my doctor told me if I didn't comply with recommended treatments, I had six months to live. You can't hear something like that and *not* change." I sipped another cool mouthful of wine. "In many ways, I'm bolder, and I wasn't exactly timid to begin with." Unconsciously, my hand tugged at the muscle shirt under my robe. "I guess I'm still a bit awkward when it comes to showing my scars."

Naomi leaned forward, opened my robe and pulled my

shirt up slowly, her eyes locked on mine the whole time. I could've stopped her. I didn't want to. When my breasts were both exposed, she studied them: first the full right breast, then the nipple-less reconstructed left breast with its horizontal scar.

"You're beautiful," she said. A quiet statement.

I could tell she meant it. It was my turn for tears.

Suddenly a cell phone rang. I was startled; I didn't think either of us had brought one into the living room and I knew I had turned mine off a while ago. She found her phone on an end table and answered the call. "Rabbi Naomi Roth," she said in a voice very different from the one that just told me my scarred breast was beautiful. In an instant, she was all business.

She got up and walked out to the sitting room while she talked, obviously seeking some privacy. As a rabbi, maybe she had to be on call for people in her congregation who had spiritual crises. I understood but had to admit I didn't like the interruption.

She returned a few minutes later and read the mild disappointment on my face. "I brought dessert," she said. "Want some?"

"I never turn down dessert!" I started to follow her into the kitchen.

"No," she said, playfully pushing me back. "It's a surprise. I'll bring it to you when it's ready."

"Can we eat it in bed?" I asked, raising my eyebrows to indicate several unspoken questions.

She grinned and returned to the kitchen.

We conducted our own very creative and tasty peach melba orgy. We managed to get peach syrup and melted ice cream in all sorts of bodily crevices, so we showered together before turning in for the night.

When we were finally in bed for the night, Naomi lay on her belly next to me. She raised herself on her elbows and whispered, "While I was traveling to all my meetings and conferences, Tess, your emails, your attention gave me a sense that you were . . . holding me in some kind of priority. I felt like someone cared. It gave me the kind of roots I didn't know I didn't have—and I could get used to it. That scares me more than a little."

"Nothing to be scared about, darling. I'm absolutely taken with you."

We slept like warm puppies, nuzzled together in contented innocence. At dawn we tried to lasso a morning star with flesh and spirit, while Chopin's "Les Adieux" played in the background.

Afterwards, she cooked me a wonderful breakfast of eggs Benedict. Again we took our meal to the living room to enjoy the ocean view. "Tell me more about this gene tracing work your organization does."

Naomi's whole being energized at the question. "It's an exciting time to be in this field! Did you know that experts have traced Thomas Jefferson's Y chromosome to the K2 line, which means he probably had a Jewish ancestor?"

"Well, no, but . . . "

She charged on, using rhetoric I realized must be part of her work presentations. "Every day we're closer to establishing a direct genetic link between an Israeli leader and a prominent Palestinian. Once those two players learn that they are 'family,' old wounds will finally begin to heal, and the Middle East will have peace."

I took an appreciative sip of the rich coffee she'd brewed for us. "But it's kind of a moot point, isn't it? I mean, don't the Jews and Arabs already agree they have a common ancestor in Abraham?"

Her enthusiasm never flickered. "Well, yes, but only in an ancient historic sense. If we can examine and trace more recent genetic histories, we can put this in familiar terms—like, 'it's true, Mr. Abbas. You and Ehud Barak are fourth cousins, five times removed.' In the Middle East, family is a potent concept. Israel would willingly share its financial wealth with its poorer Palestinian brothers . . . "

I jumped in. "It didn't do much for Obama and his 'cousin' Cheney. If you think that finding a genetic link between Abraham's warring offspring will lead to world peace, you have a case of idealism not curable by penicillin or cynicism, and only mitigated by witticism."

She laughed but broke eye contact. "I've raised hundreds of thousands of dollars for this cause. I love my work, Tess."

Something in her voice told me it would be wiser to find other things to tease her about.

We lingered so long we had just enough time to shower, pack our bags and kiss good-bye before check-out time. We both took a calla lily home.

On the drive back to San Diego, I concurred with Satchmo: it's a wonderful world. I felt hopeful and invigorated. I also felt higher than the U.S. trade deficit. Intimacy with Naomi altered my state of consciousness. I'd known passion before. I'd known lust. I'd known tenderness. I'd known care, concern, even real love. But never before had I experienced such a deep hormonal, pheromonal and psychological intoxication; I'd never before drunk of such amygdala ambrosia.

In *Alice in Wonderland* the caterpillar asks Alice, "Who are you?" Alice replies, "I hardly know, sir, just at present—at least I know who I was when I got up this morning, but I think I must have been changed several times since then."

In Laguna, I fell through the Looking Glass.

22

TINKERING WITH SUSPECTS

"I'VE BEEN ARRESTED!"

Like a frog's tongue with a fly, the panic in Beth's voice flicked out and zapped my attention away from the luscious ponderings about Naomi I had entertained on my grocery run, and brought my focus back to the New Mexico murder. "What happened?"

Through sniffs and sobs, Beth related her tale. Kendra's sister Caitlin had hooked up with the son of a New Mexico state senator through Facebook. Whether odd coincidence or specific intention, Beth didn't know. Caitlin pressured her new boyfriend who, in turn, pressured his senator father, who (you guessed it) pressured the District Attorney's office in Socorro, the sheriff in Catron County, and anyone else he could lean on. Their argument, from Caitlin on down was: It's been almost two months since Kendra was killed. Only one person had a weapon at the Lightning Field with which to commit the murder. Why haven't you arrested her?

Then Lyle's psychiatrist threw Crisco on the barbee. He issued a medical-legal report stating the reason for Lyle's suicide attempt was grief, not guilt. The shrink's report upped the ante, and a warrant for Beth's arrest had been signed by the district judge in Catron County.

"The Albuquerque cops dragged me off to Catron County to be arraigned. Let me tell you, that was fun," Beth said with vinegar in her voice. "But eventually they let me come back to Albuquerque where my very pricey attorney, who Bryce is paying for, thank God, arranged my release on a million dollars' bail. My attorney said if I wasn't pregnant, I'd probably be in jail. Me, 'out on bail!' Never thought I'd say those words, Tess. And I was lucky to get bail. The authorities were nervous about whether they could provide the right medical care if anything happened to the baby . . . " Beth's voice cracked as anger succumbed to fear.

I tried to calm her. "You're no more a murderer than I am the Dalai Lama. No jury would convict you. Have you heard from Armida?"

"Her hands are tied, Tess." Sniffles. "I have to wear this stupid ankle monitor even when I sleep. I can't leave Albuquerque. I, I . . . " She sobbed herself into another meltdown.

A nurse once told me that when a woman is PMS, that's when her hormone levels are closest to those of men. Which explains why, during our most challenging days, we act the way some men act normally—cantankerous, with little impulse control. If PMS can make us act like the guys on the Jackass show, Beth's prenatal hormones put her on the same even keel as the Unabomber. "Maybe you shouldn't be alone, Beth. Are you allowed to have someone there with you?"

"Yes, my sister Katie's coming from Wisconsin for a stay."

I promised Beth I'd renew my sleuthing efforts and signed off.

When I got home, Lana was in the back yard watering the many herbs, flowers, shrubs, and trees she bonds with out there. After giving Raj and Pookie their props, I filled Lana in on Beth's arrest.

"She's what—five months pregnant now? She must be terrified. What can we do to help?"

I appreciated the "we." I also appreciated there was very little Lana could do. She was involved in her usual medley of massage clients, Tai chi classes, and herb workshops, as well as her relationship with Gable.

The sweet scent from late-blooming roses in the garden reminded me of the long-stemmed beauties Naomi sent me recently. These past five weeks, we'd spent as much time together as her schedule would allow. Now, I fought the urge to slide back through the Looking Glass; the despair I'd heard in Beth's voice helped me focus. "There is one thing you could help with, when you're not in the middle of all this." I gestured at the garden. "I'm trying to piece together strips of shredded documents. They belonged to Ned Merkur. There's a chance they'll provide a clue."

I didn't tell Lana that this task had about the same chance of helping us solve the murder that I have of falling in love with Ann Coulter. Nevertheless, the shredded documents were worth a try; I didn't have much else to work with. I retreated to my bedroom, Raj at my heels, mulling over Beth's arrest and the Lightning Field murder.

Means, motive, and opportunity are the keys, right? It was possible that someone had crept into the room Beth and I shared at the cabin, taken her Taser, and returned it after the murder. Or that someone at the Lightning Field had successfully hidden a Taser or cattle prod somewhere. Or that Jorge or the ranger had brought a weapon in, then departed with it. Given these unlikely but not impossible scenarios, "means" was a moot point. All of my suspects could have had means. "Opportunity" levied more suspicion on Ned, Rashid, and Lyle than the ranger or Jorge. And motive? Motive was as elusive as Britney Spears's inner adult. Armida had run background checks, studied bank records, and personally interviewed each suspect. As far as Armida or I could tell, no one had any connection to Kendra before the Lightning Field visit except Lyle.

I took out my Tinker Toys; they help me think. I selected a large double-grooved hub piece. It looked important, so I designated it the Kendra piece. What other pieces would fit into that hub? Raj gave me his curious, wrinkled-brow look.

I connected a straight yellow rod to a notched wooden spool to represent Lyle, who currently had a notch in his head. Lyle was still under medical care. Armida would have told me if anything suspicious had been discovered at his apartment or bike shop. He could be lying to his shrink, but anyone willing to put a bullet in his own head was probably past the point of conniving. I considered him a lukewarm suspect at best. I set my Lyle Tinker Toy construct aside.

I chose two shorter blue rods linked by an orange plastic connector for Ned, because the blue reminded me of his eyes and the orange was as close as I could come to the butterscotch color of his hair. I'd spent time with Ned, and while he was definitely a colorful character, I didn't sense anything malicious in him. In fact, I liked him. The Tinker Toy figure I designated "Ned" would remain near the Kendra hub, but not connected to it, not yet anyway.

A long beige rod topped by a beige spool served as Park Ranger George Calvert. I chose generic beige because I didn't know much about him, other than that Armida liked him. I couldn't think of any reason why he'd want to murder a woman he'd only known for fifteen minutes but I felt some suspicion about the ranger. The evening he arrived at the Lightning Field, Lyle and Kendra had stayed on the front porch when the rest of us went to greet him. Calvert had asked pointedly if we were "all present." At the time it seemed he was merely a conscientious ranger who wanted everyone to hear his warning about mountain lions. But what if, for reasons unknown, his mountain lion warning was merely a pretext to verify Kendra's presence there? Too many questions; not enough answers. I put Ranger Calvert's pieces aside.

Two red rods joined by a green plastic connector —two of the colors of the Mexican flag—worked for Jorge. Jorge had a criminal record, although not for a violent crime. He had skipped the country and was wanted for questioning by the New Mexican authorities. He might be involved with Kendra's murder, but any detecting on my part was stalled, since I didn't have the resources to go south of the border to find him. I laid the Jorge Tinker Toy figure near the hub. Certainly couldn't rule him out, but didn't have any grounds—yet—for linking him with Kendra.

That left one Tinker Toy character. I inserted a green plastic flag piece into the slit on a spool, and connected the spool to a blue rod. "The soft-spoken, observant Rashid is perhaps not what he seems," I told my handsome terrier. "Green, beige, blue—what are Rashid's true colors? I hereby promise you, myself, and Beth's unborn bundle that I'll track him down."

Raj approved of my determination by chewing on Lyle's notched head.

A little background on Rashid would definitely help. The more I knew about him, the easier it would be to question him. My dearly beloved ex-husband, Roark, worked for a powerful spook organization and could access voluminous inside information, so I called him for help. To my surprise, he flat-out refused. He brought up a lot of irrelevant old history that pissed me off. "Sorry, little darlin'; I'm not gonna contribute to your delinquency. You think playing detective is some kind of game. I made the mistake of cooperating with you before and you nearly got yourself killed. Not this time, unh uh."

"But Roark, in both cases I solved the murders! Doesn't that justify the risk?"

"There's a perfectly competent investigator for the district attorney on this case. I talked to her when you gave me as a reference. She seems quite capable, sweet cheeks. I don't need my ex-wife found bludgeoned or broiled somewhere in the wilds of New Mexico. You keep your nose outta this one."

So much for Roark as resource. Ah, well, my spirits were soon boosted.

From: fem_reb@pccoalition.org
To: freepi4all@gmail.com
Darling Tess, Here I am in my hotel room, trying to focus on a speech for tomorrow's big event. But my mind wanders to your stroke with the calla lily; the funny growl you do when you're really excited. . . .

Do you have any idea how you have liberated me sexually—and what a tremendous gift that is? You seem uniquely suited to give me what I've always known I wanted but didn't have the vocabulary to describe. I love how you make me feel—what you give me safety to express. Whatever this is between us, G-d is in it. If we are trusting of that—and loving of each other—all will be well. And that's as theological as I'll get until I see you, when (knowing you), I'll be panting "Oh, G-d" frequently!
xxxx, Naomi

From: freepi4all@gmail.com
To: fem_reb@pccoalition.org
Wish you were in town, sweetheart, and not off at the Boulder fundraiser, because I'll be in the City of Angels tomorrow to question a man who was at the Lightning Field with me. My pregnant friend Beth's been arrested and I need to do everything I can to help solve the murder.

I love you forty degrees past what's circumspect, a little to the right of my pillow, and two notches beyond what I thought I was capable of. I feel Shalom in your arms.
Tess

23

HOW YOU SEE IT; HOW YOU DON'T

THE NEXT DAY I WAS behind the wheel of the Silver Bullet at an intersection in downtown L.A., listening to Double Helixx, a Philly band, thumping out the rhythm of "Crossfire" on my steering wheel. A guy driving a red Eclipse pulled up next to me and began finger-drilling one nostril. I watched him as we both waited at a red light. He turned and saw me, glanced away and continued to mine for mucus. I've seen guys do it dozens of times, somehow believing a car provided them invisibility or social cover. Good thing the light changed when it did, because I didn't want to know what he did with the booger when he retrieved it.

Alliance Security Insurance Company claimed the fifth, sixth, and seventh floors of an office building on South Main. The receptionist's name plate read WILLIAMS GERSHON. Williams seemed a pleasant enough Gen Z queen whose blatant bling somehow worked with his curly black hair. He looked up from a lurid graphic novel. "May I help you?"

"I need to speak to one of your fraud investigators—Rashid Prince?"

A peculiar look crossed his face. He smoothed what remained of his plucked eyebrows. "Mr. Prince is not in. I can take a message for you, or one of our other representatives would be glad to assist you."

"No, this is a personal legal matter," I said, skirting dangerously close to the truth. I'd have to stop that before it became a habit. I leaned in toward Williams and whispered, "Look, my client's pursuing a nasty matter involving paternity tests and child support," I said, implying I was a lawyer without ever saying it. "I understand Mr. Prince already has a family. If I could just speak with him briefly, maybe we can settle this thing out of court before it gets coyote ugly. When is he expected?"

Eyebrows tamed, his nervous fingers now tugged at the five drill bits in his left ear. "Mr. Prince is out on medical leave."

Red alert, red alert! "Was he in an accident or something?"

"Uh, he had a heart attack. Right here at work."

"How long ago was this?"

Williams consulted his desk calendar. "Three days."

"What hospital is he in?"

"Ma'am, I can't give out that kind of information. Why don't you leave a message on Mr. Prince's voice mail? I'm sure he'll get back to you when he feels better."

"You related to Gina Gershon?"

"No, but there is a resemblance, isn't there?" Williams was still smiling to himself as I walked out.

Damn. I paid $4.50 parking for this?

I wondered if Rashid had been poisoned; the symptoms from certain poisons could mimic a heart attack. In the August heat, I walked back to my car where I retrieved my laptop and hoofed it over to a Starbuck's on West Sixth. I ordered an iced chai, sat down and called the Los Angeles Fire Department. I asked them where the paramedics had taken the heart attack victim from Alliance Security three days ago. After a blitz of bureaucracy, rationalizing, two follow-up calls and blatant social engineering, I learned there was no record of a 911 call for any heart attack victim at that address on that day. I asked them to check several days before and after. Nada.

Ned was right: Rashid had to be a spook. His employment with the insurance company was a cover. Time for Plan B.

I booted my laptop and went online. Hadn't Ned said Rashid's wife worked as an optician? The Opticians Association of America web site had a membership directory—one with a Search function, no less. I didn't know Rashid's wife's name, but I entered Prince as the last name and L.A. for the location. Within seconds I found what I was looking for: Mrs. Riko Prince worked at Vision Advantages in the 4700 block of Venice Boulevard. I took my iced chai with me.

Minutes later I entered a one-story yellow stucco building. Behind the counter an older Asian man sat hunched over a pile of paperwork. "May I speak to Mrs. Prince, please?"

"You have appointment?"

"No, it's kind of a surprise. A good surprise." I smiled and tried to look like I might represent a very mature American Idol scout.

He motioned me down a hallway. "Two doors, on right."

The door was leaned to. I pushed it open and entered. Suddenly, eye of newt, eye of Horus, eye of Sauron, and eye of the hurricane all stared up at me! Brown and blue and hazel eyeballs; big and medium and smaller eyeballs, seventeen in all. Criminitlies! The prosthetic eyeballs lay in a plastic tray on a cart. They watched me unblinkingly, following my every move like the eyes of a plastic Jesus hologram. At least that's how it felt.

An attractive Asian woman in her thirties wearing tight jeans and a short-sleeved aqua lab smock held something small against a buffing machine. When she looked up, she greeted me. "Oh, hi! Can I help you?"

I took my own eyes off the artificial eyes and extended my hand. "I'm Tess Camillo. Are you Riko Prince?"

"Yes . . . "

"I met your husband Rashid at the Lightning Field in New Mexico."

Her manner grew guarded. I tried not to stare at the artificial eyes, but it was like trying not to looky-loo at a head-on collision when you pass it on the road. Riko noticed my discomfiture.

"They won't hurt you," she said gently.

"It's just that I wasn't expecting them. Eyeglasses and contact lenses, maybe. But I never realized . . . "

"It's a subspecialty for opticians, requiring certification. I work with a variety of ocular prosthetics, both artificial eyes and scleral shells. Since the Iraq War, there's been greater need."

Suddenly, I saw the seventeen eyeballs in a different way. I glanced around at her work area. An expensive-looking computer, monitor flashing a screen saver of jasmine blossoms. A wall calendar from a Vail ski resort. A work bench with assorted grinding and polishing machines and spray cans. Metal trays holding something that looked like shiny white dough. The smell of paint and plastics. And everywhere, framed photos of a cute dark-haired boy. "Ah, that's Ramo."

She couldn't help but smile at her own progeny. "Yes, I suppose Rashid told you about him?"

"He's a proud father, all right."

"What do you want, Ms. Camillo?" A line of perspiration appeared on her upper lip, despite the air conditioning.

"I need to talk to your husband. I went to the Alliance Security office." I looked at her meaningfully. "I don't think I'll find him there, do you?"

"Sorry, I can't help you." She inserted an artificial eyeball into a measuring device and jotted down some readings.

I held out one of Ramo's pictures. "Mrs. Prince, a dear friend of mine who's in her forties is five months pregnant by in vitro fertilization. She's wanted a child her entire adult life. And now she's accused of the murder that took place while your husband was at the Lightning Field. The stress of that puts her in danger of losing the baby." I paused for effect. "Can you imagine your life without Ramo?"

She blinked several times and grew very still.

I continued, "Look, I know your husband works for Homeland Security or the CIA or something, right? I'm not trying to blow the lid off of any national secrets; I just want to ask him a few questions."

"I'll take a break." Riko locked up her workshop and we walked around the block.

Outside, the humidity made it hard to breathe. "Rashid

didn't visit the Lightning Field to improve his sketching, did he?" I began.

"No."

"He was on assignment?"

She stopped in the middle of the sidewalk and studied my face. "Your friend is really in danger of losing her baby?"

"Ask Rashid. He met her at the Lightning Field; her name is Beth."

She made an assessment of me and continued our walk. "Rashid works for the FBI on money laundering cases. He was attempting an undercover investigation of a man named Ned. He'd be furious with me if he knew I told you this."

"He won't know. Did you ever hear Rashid mention a woman named Kendra? Her married name is Kendra Theisman; her maiden name was Billings."

"Only when he told me about the murder out there."

"You never heard him mention her before, like maybe someone he once dated?"

She shrugged her shoulders. "Rashid dated a lot of girls in high school and college; I don't remember all their names. I can't help you."

"Mrs. Prince, I know this is a personal question and maybe a painful one, but I have to ask. Could your husband have been having an affair?"

"Could he? Yes. He travels a lot. But I dated quite a bit before marrying, too. I knew what I was looking for in a husband. Rashid's not the cheating type."

"Where is he now?"

"Reno, I think. Another undercover assignment. It's not easy . . ."

"I see."

I'd made one more bad vision pun but little progress. Ned's obfuscation on his 1040's had apparently pissed off the Feds, who wondered if his never-profitable Off the Map museum was a front for money laundering. But Ned had not been arrested and Rashid had been pulled off the case. The FBI apparently had bigger locusts to roast.

I was pretty damned certain Rashid wasn't going to make himself available to me for questioning. Damn, another dead end, or at least one that needed life support.

On the way home, I hit a bumper-to-bumper stretch in Irvine and phoned Armida. "You knew about Rashid, didn't you?" I asked.

"What are you talking about, Tess?"

"He's FBI. He was assigned to crawl up Ned's butt; see if he's involved with money laundering."

"OK, I'm not sure how you found out, but yes, I knew."

"Why didn't you tell me? I thought we were collaborators."

"I couldn't break an agent's cover just because you were curious or worried about Beth." Armida sighed with frustration. "That said, I've done some discreet probing and I don't see anything in Rashid's background or personal life that would give him a motive to kill Kendra Theisman. His assignment to Ned at the Lightning Field was a last-minute thing. In fact, he told police he almost missed the van ride out to the Field."

"Yes, I remember; he was running late. Was Rashid carrying a Taser?"

"No. He did have a Glock 23 on him, standard issue for FBI agents. But no electrical weapon; nothing that could've inflicted the wounds we found on Kendra. Rashid identified himself to Sheriff Garcia as FBI. And he surrendered all his belongings for a thorough search which, frankly, was very cooperative for a Fibby."

"Damn, where does that leave us?"

"It leaves Beth under arrest. I'll keep in touch."

I was sure behind the eyeball, er, eight ball, with this murder investigation.

24

RAIDERS OF THE LOST ARCH

LANA ASKED ME TO LET her tell you this part of the story, so here goes . . .

Ever since Tess hooked up with this Naomi, I've been concerned for her. I'm not jealous; I've got Gable in my life. It's just that Tess doesn't quite seem like her old self lately. I know she's concerned about what our friendship will be like when I get married, so I've been trying to show her she's still important to me.

She wants to solve this Lightning Field murder, and to be supportive, in my free time I help her piece together these little strippy-doos of shredded documents. I'm not sure how these documents tie into the murder of the young woman at the Lightning Field, but Tess seems to think they could be important.

This morning we were hunched over the dining room

table, trying to piece these things back together. Tess likes to do them in the morning because she says the strong light is easier on her eyes. She tries to match words from one strip to words on another. I do it a different way: I look at the shapes and patterns of the paper, rather than what's written on them. Tess says there are no differences in the strips because they all went through the same shredder, but I've matched just as many pieces as she has.

We were working on these strippy-doos almost the whole morning. I know it's important because her friend Beth has been arrested, but I was getting bored. I started to daydream about where Gable and I might have our wedding ceremony. It has to be some place outdoors; both of us love nature.

"It's been twenty minutes since you've matched a piece," Tess pointed out. "Anything wrong?"

She always has a clock going off in her brain. I'm sure the tick, tick, tick gets tiresome. "I could use a break," I told her as I stretched and then bent down to scratch dear Pookie's head.

Tess furrowed her brow as she tried to match words from strip A to strip B.

"I've got an idea!" I said.

"And what might that be?"

"Yesterday I used the internet to look for . . . "

"Wait, wait, wait! *You* used the internet? You never go online. That's like Bush saying he 'used the Google.'"

Sometimes Tess enjoys poking fun at me. I didn't let it perturb me one bit. "Yes, I did go on the internet. Gable and I were at the Encinitas library. While the librarian helped him with something, I used one of their computers to go online. I found a beautiful landmark in Balboa Park called the Cheren Arch where Gable and I could say our vows. The web site said the arch was symbolic of love, romance, and marriage, and that couples who pass through the arch together will have a flawless wedding."

"A flawless wedding is a contradiction in terms," Tess replied.

Sometimes she can be a real booger. Well, so can I. I know she's concerned about the weight she gained in New Mexico, so I tossed in the word "exercise." "You know, we both could use some exercise; let's take Raj and Pookie to Balboa Park and check out the Cheren Arch."

We grabbed the dogs, the leashes, and the photo of the Arch I'd printed from the Internet, and went out into the gorgeous day.

By the time we got to the park, my chi felt clearer. I led the way into the park starting at the museums. No sign of the Cheren Arch there. We wandered into a marvelous grove of pepper trees, eucalyptus, acacia, and palms. "Oh, isn't this enchanting! Maybe we could get married right here."

Tess looked at me. "I'm not so sure these trees wouldn't ruin the whole ceremony. You see, birds sit on tree branches—birds who may not be properly potty trained. Do you really want birds showering down their aromatic little parcels on your wedding guests?"

Sometimes I can't believe how her mind works. "Don't be crude, Tess."

A jet passed overhead on its approach to Lindbergh Field. I forgot how low they fly along here. The noise caused disturbance in three of my chakras. Maybe this wasn't the right spot. We continued our search for the Cheren Arch.

Dogs in tow, we soon found ourselves at the edge of a brick restaurant patio featuring a wishing well, Mexican food, and margaritas. We were thirsty so we sat down and ordered iced teas. I asked the waiter if he could direct us to the stone arch in the picture I'd printed off the internet. Darling Pookie loved the waiter's trouser smells and was getting perhaps a bit too cozy with the waiter's leg.

"I haven't seen this arch," the waiter said, shaking Pookie off his cuff. "Try the south side of the park where there are more historical structures."

When we finished our drinks, we headed south past a puppet theater. Raj and Pookie stopped in their tracks, bewildered to see small renditions of something that looked like people dancing around. But these things didn't smell or sound like people, so it really confused them. They skittered out of the way of the quickly moving sticks with funny eyes and oversized painted shoes.

We proceeded to a garden area near the United Nations International Houses. The flower beds had all been freshly manicured and I felt rich with the moment.

Probably because she's so taken by Rabbi Naomi, Tess steered us toward the House of Israel. Raj and Pookie kept glancing over their shoulders, wary of the weird dancing puppets that might reappear.

"I have to admit, Tess, I never pictured you with a rabbi. What exactly is it about Naomi that so captivates you? Are you fascinated with her personality? The fact that she's a clergy member?" I didn't say "her sex appeal?" I know Tess well enough that I was sure that played a big role, whether she admitted it or not. After all, we were once lovers.

"It's hard to put into words, Lana," she responded. "Until I met Naomi, I didn't realize I was like this but . . . When I see a good-looking woman all prim and proper, maybe wearing a business suit and her hair's up in a bun, something inside of me really, really wants to un-bun her, if you know what I mean."

I fought back a smile. I'd sensed this trait in Tess a long time ago.

"I want to make her go crazy, make her shake her hair out all loose and wild. Some powerful button in me gets pushed . . . " She looked at me to see if I was following. "I told you it was hard to explain."

"So her aloofness is a challenge?"

"Right, that's part of it. She's also smart. And very passionate." Pookie had tangled her leash around Tess' legs, forcing her to pause for a moment and unwrap. "You've met her, Lana. You've seen her charisma. You admit she's attractive, right? Someone you'd want to know better?"

I wasn't about to tell Tess what I really thought of Naomi. It wasn't fair; I'd only spent a few minutes around her, when I was coming and going at the house during some of her visits—not even long enough to pick up on her aura. But something about her seemed off to me. Like I noticed that her mouth smiles a lot more than her eyes do. And the dogs didn't warm up to her; they kept their distance. Naomi certainly didn't seem like this loving, passionate person Tess believed her to be, but I kept my opinion to myself. "You and I are different, Tess; we probably see different things in people."

She let it go. Still no sign of the Arch, the white quartz archway that seemed the perfect wedding location. "Let's head back to the Prado and ask the Balboa Park administrative office where it is."

By the time we got there, the midday heat was sapping our energy.

Tess asked the first person she met at the front desk, an older fellow with royal blue suspenders. "Well, Miss, now this is an interesting problem," he began. "I'm a retired archaeologist; worked the Copan ruins down in Honduras. Now there was a dig . . . "

Tess cut him off. "This arch we're looking for has the word Cheren written right on it. Surely you must know where . . . "

The retired archaeologist began telling Tess about dinosaur bones he discovered at some site. "Guess you could call me a real boner, heh, heh, heh . . . "

Tess' aura was turning red, so I intervened. "This is what we're looking for," I said, pointing to the picture on the web page. "It's a landmark. I found it on the San Diego Historical Society's web site."

The fellow studied the photo but shook his head. "Haven't seen anything like this in Balboa Park, and I've worked here most of my seventy-seven years."

Tess asked the other admin staff about it. Everyone said the same thing: they'd never seen the Cheren Arch.

I felt really discouraged. We walked by an ice cream stand that carried one of my favorite flavors, green tea, and gave in to temptation. Tess found us a bench to sit on next to the botanical gardens' lily pond. As we ate, we watched koi dart into corners and dragonflies flutter over lily pads.

Halfway through her caramel cone Tess asked, "How did you know—absolutely, for sure—that Gable was the right one for you?"

I slid my tongue along the green ice cream and thought about my fiancé. Tender silly things popped into my mind. Like that little crinkle right above his ear lobes. The freckles on his shoulders that always make me smile. How safe I feel when he's driving. I knew those weren't the things Tess wanted to hear about, so I sat up straight and began to pinpoint the important characteristics that set him apart. "Something in his smile reflected his innermost core. It anchored me to him; telling me it would be safe to give him a chance—if he wanted that chance."

Tess looked at me attentively. "Anchored you to him. What's that mean exactly?"

I dug deeper within, revealing more of my feelings to Tess than I had in a long time. "I believe that it was a true heart connection, a vibrational harmony. Right from the start, Gable seemed genuinely interested in me—what my favorite flower was, what my dreams were . . . "

Tess squirmed. I hoped she didn't hear these remarks as a condemnation of our relationship years ago. We made much better friends than we had lovers. I licked a drip of ice cream from the side of my cone and continued. "I had his natal chart done when I first met him. He's one of my favorite signs—a highly intelligent Libra with sensitive Pisces rising—just a dream-pie!" Tess hasn't yet opened her mind to astrology. "As I spent time with Gable, I found him centered, generous, flirtatious, but not invasive or forceful. He listened to me, to my heart and to my mind. Can any of us share our innermost selves unless we feel safe? Something about him did that for me."

Both dogs were now rolling on their backs and yipping, begging for ice cream. We pretended to ignore them. I continued, "I kept waiting for Gable to slip up, to show some significant flaws, but I still haven't found much except . . . "

"Except what?"

"Well, lately he's been pressuring me about going back to school and 'doing something' with my life. I told him the one thing I want to 'do' with my life is live it."

Tess looked at me more intently. Raj caught some difference in our body language and began to wag his tail, sure that we had decided to share our cones.

"Oh, we're not in any real trouble. Gable means well; our culture puts strange demands on men—demands about achievement and money and success, and sometimes he lets those negative expectations flow toward me. Most of the time, though, he's a dear and loving man. It's been, what? Five months now . . . I can hardly imagine my life without him."

My intuition told me that Tess was trying to apply all of this to her own circumstances. "Do you know what it is you're really looking for this time around, Tess? Have you spent time examining your inner self, to discover what works and what doesn't work for you on this journey we all make?" We both looked out over the reflecting pond. "Are there special qualities in a partner that make you want to dance like a dragonfly over lily pads?"

"Sometimes I'm *more* than that happy with Naomi. Other times, well, she's complex . . . "

"Why not give it some time? The relationship with Naomi

will either be there for a season, a reason, or a lifetime. Remember to see her with your heart's vision." I glanced down at the lovely Akoya Japanese pearl and diamond engagement ring Gable had given me. I really wanted to find this Cheren Arch. I pulled out the web page with the picture and re-read the information.

"There must be some clue in the photo about where the Arch is located. Maybe something in the shadows? There's a tree on the left . . . " I handed the web page to Tess.

She scrutinized the web page carefully. Suddenly I saw a smile skitter across her face. "Lana, how did you find this web page?"

"I went on the internet. I searched Google for 'wedding' and 'arch' and 'Balboa Park' so I could find a really cool place for the wedding. Why do you ask?"

"See this URL at the top of the page?"

I squinted at a line of alphabet soup web address gunk. "So?"

"This isn't from the San Diego Historical Society; it's from a web site called the San Diego *Hysterical* Society!" Tess quoted from the page, "'Constructed of a unique ochre alabaster now known as Cheren-stone, the arch gives off a soft golden glow . . . ' 'Cheren-stone.' Sharon Stone. Get it? Lana, this whole thing's a spoof!"

We looked at each other and melted into laughter. Whatever tensions we'd felt in our talk about Naomi and Gable, at this moment in the warm San Diego sun, we were just two old friends laughing ourselves silly. Raj and Pookie licked the last drips of ice cream from the sidewalk. They didn't worry too much about finding perfect relationships; they took pleasure in the ones they had.

25

STARDUST

"THERE I WAS IN the Lightning Field cabin. Kendra's body was lying dead on the floor. Ants crawled all over her, just like they did when we first discovered the murder."

Lana sat across from me in the breakfast nook, chasing the last blueberry in her bowl of yogurt. Hummingbirds sipped nectar from the feeder that hung outside in our patio. Lemon sunshine poured in through the windows, promising a perfect beach day. My friend Tiger and I planned to sail her catamaran around Mission Bay in the afternoon.

Lana and I had just finished breakfast and had cleared most of the table for the tedious task of piecing together what she calls strippy-doos. I laid out several pairs of tweezers, Scotch tape and a magnifying glass. So far our cumulative efforts amounted to half of one taped-together page and three-quarters of another. I knew Lana would bail on me if she got bored, so I tried to make last night's dream as intriguing as possible.

Lana seemed interested in the tale. "And then what happened?"

"Well, this doesn't make sense, but you know how dreams are. For some reason, these ants had personalities and could speak. I was assigned to vacuum up the ants from around Kendra. I did, but three of them hid in a corner and escaped. One claimed he was an evangelist. He preached to the other two about the Apocalypse; said all the prophesies foretold of Death by Vacuum in the Final Days if ants didn't repent of their 'ant-ics'!"

"What do you think your subconscious is trying to tell you with that dream?"

"Well, I get the obvious symbolism—I mean, hey, a vacuum? Yes, Death sucks. Murder sucks. And religion? I'm dating a rabbi. But how does entomology fit in?" I looked forward to sharing the peculiar little dream with Naomi, who had returned from Boulder and was driving down from L.A. to see me that night. "I had another dream, too . . . "

"Tess, look!" Lana's expression looked like she had swallowed bumblebees. She handed me a taped-together page of document strips and pointed to one particular line of text.

I read it. "Kendra! Ned knew Kendra Theisman!" I was so excited I nearly knocked my toast crust off the table. Raj smiled and informed me that would not, at all, be a problem.

Within ten minutes my enthusiasm had fizzled. No evidence of an adulterous affair. No secret cabal of people who get their jollies titillating one another with dangerous electrical devices. No blackmail. Nothing half so thrilling. The page with Kendra's name on it was part of a membership roster for an income tax reform group Ned had founded. Kendra had joined, but apparently so had hundreds, maybe thousands, of others.

Still, income tax trouble was what put away Al Capone; it might have some significance. I phoned Armida to tell her. "Right, I can clearly read Kendra's name and address, along with a checkbox indicating her interest in tax reform. Looks like the organization had a considerable membership list."

Armida mused, "I wonder why Ned shredded it?"

"Ned's paranoid about the Feds. He's skating on thin ice with his income tax. He'd figured Rashid for a spook. He probably came home from the Lightning Field and shredded a lot of paper records, while squirreling away digital copies somewhere. It fits with Ned's mentality perfectly, but it doesn't bring us any closer to solving Kendra's murder."

Raj nudged my leg, wanting a walk. The glorious weather beckoned to him, too.

"I've had another idea," I told Armida. "They probably took photos during Kendra's autopsy. Could a forensics expert state, definitively, whether her wounds were made by a Taser or by a cattle prod? If we could rule out Beth's Taser as the murder weapon, maybe they'd release her . . ."

"Sorry, Tess," Armida replied, "I already looked into that. The medical examiner said multiple wounds were inflicted, one on top of the other. Determining the exact the shape or size of the electrical contacts of the murder weapon was just not possible."

Discouraged, I hung up. In the living room, Lana had embarked on a new project. Piles of her clothing—a stack of jeans here, another of tee shirts or skirts there—covered the floor in front of the living room fireplace as well as most of the sofa and all of the coffee table.

I carefully filed the taped-together pages of Ned's tax organization list, then watched Lana for a few minutes. She would pick an item from a pile (presumably from an emptied dresser drawer), examine it, drift around the room with it, sometimes stopping to water plants or play with Pookie, then she'd place the item into one of three cardboard boxes, or she'd return it to the pile. Sometimes her discernment process involved smelling the piece of clothing. I knew that in her mind, there was method to this madness. "What're you up to?"

Lana held a fuzzy pink sweater up for final scrutiny, and placed it in a cardboard box on her right. "Donating some old clothes to Goodwill. If I move in with Gable, well, his house has small closets."

I took note of the "If" and not "when." Interesting. She looked up from a pair of green denim hip huggers. "You said you had another dream last night. What was it?"

"I dreamt I was in a bar, shooting pool and cruising women. At first I wasn't paying much attention to the game. Then I looked down to make a shot and realized the pool balls were all eyeballs, rolling around on the table."

Lana, who didn't know I'd recently visited a vision prosthetics lab, offered complex interpretations of the dream, including that I might need to go on a "vision quest." Oy.

She eventually abandoned her clothing project and prepared to meet a massage client. She lugged her massage table toward the front door. "After this appointment, I'm heading to Gable's for the night. You and Naomi have the place to yourselves."

I helped her lift the table into the back of her truck and hugged her good-bye. As soon as I stepped back in the house, my brother in Jersey called. "Hey, Baron, what's new?" I made small talk while I frantically searched the living room for the notes I kept on our phone conversations. I found them under a blue and turquoise scarf on an end table. My eyes scanned the notes from his Africa conversation: melons in Lilongwe, rides in park ranger's paraglider, giraffe at hotel windows.

"You'll never guess what happened, Sis, you'll never guess!" The Baron sounded like a peacock tail looks. Had his auto dealership just sold their 5,000th Lexus?

"If I'll never guess, you'd better just tell me."

"Carole and I went to Bally's casino last night and won a shit load of money!"

"How many pesos in a shit load, *mi hermano*?" I removed colorful skirts from a cushion of the cream-colored leather sofa and sat down.

"One hundred and ten thousand bucks!"

The Baron needed money like I needed an extra twenty pounds. "Jeez, Baron, they'll probably never let you into Bally's again. What was it—blackjack?"

"Roulette! Tess, can you believe it?"

I could believe it because I knew what Tolstoy knew: there's scant justice in our fractured little corner of the universe. Whatever justice there was, I wanted for Kendra. And Beth.

I let the Baron brag and ramble, then decided to wrap things up. "Hey, I'm happy for you, bro. Oh, got another call coming in. Take care."

After I hung up, I wrote "Bally's, $110,000, roulette" on the note page. Something in the earlier notes caught my eye: park ranger's paraglider. Could Ranger Calvert have waited until the storm ended at the Lightning Field, then glided in quietly, entered the cabin, and murdered Kendra? Did New Mexico park rangers have access to paragliders like the ones my brother's family had seen in Africa? Could you even fly those things at night? And if you could, why on earth would Ranger Calvert want to murder Kendra? Maybe this paraglider thing was a bum lead. It seemed far-fetched so I filed it in the back-40 of my brain for another time.

I had a full day ahead of me. I'd do a quick work out at Curves, then meet Tiger in Mission Bay Park for our sail at two-thirty. And in the evening I had to attend a job networking career thing at the Marriott. I hated those events, but all the major employers who hire database programmers in San Diego would be there. And I'd have Naomi to look forward to when I returned. She was still 120 miles away, but I could feel an anticipation buzz coming on.

That night when I arrived home I immediately knew something was up. Naomi's Prius was parked out front but the house was dark. Hmm. I'd told Naomi where Lana and I hid the extra key so she could let herself in. She should be greeting me at the door. Where was she?

I used my own key to enter. The rich melancholy cello of "Flames" by Vast emanated from the back of the house, where I detected a faint light. I switched on a living room lamp so I could maneuver around the Goodwill garment obstacle course, and walked down the hall toward my room.

Naomi was lying on her back in the middle of the bed, head propped up on a pillow so she could see my reaction. She wore nothing but the no-longer-stained beige satin robe, which hung open. A thick scented candle flickered and dripped melted wax into a holder positioned between her spread legs.

As I approached, I noticed something else: Naomi's skin glistened in the candle light. "What the . . . ?" I was too dazzled to speak.

"It's glitter," she explained. "The stuff the kids wear to mosh pits. I'm covered with it." Naomi's eyes and the tone in her voice told me that, despite seventeen years of marriage, this seduction was very new territory for her.

She must've brought a homemade CD of romantic songs; Madeleine Peyroux now sang "No More." As the candlelight caught the glitter, subtle sparks danced across Naomi's belly, over her breasts, and down her thighs, lending a magical allure. Sandalwood scent permeated the room.

An intense desire flushed through me. Assertively I removed the candle from between her legs and placed it on the nearby dresser. Without a word I pulled my clothes off and lunged onto the bed. We swam through a viscous sensuality, as one song after another sent subliminal code to our hearts. The glitter that started out on her soon decorated both of our entwined bodies.

"Tell me what you want, baby," I urged.

She wasn't good at telling yet, but she showed me while Rufus Wainwright crooned his sensitive rendition of Leonard Cohen's "Hallelujah." The sweet animal in me nipped, purred and thundered in synch with the sweet animal in her. Deep within her, my fingers recognized a certain tensing and pulsing . . .

And from her lips I drew her hallelujah.

26

AZIMUTH

THE NEXT MORNING I got up, set some java a-brewing, then returned to bed where Naomi and I watched CNN and snuggled. During commercials we talked about my career networking meeting (boring) and yesterday's catamaran ride (a refreshing rush and a sunburned nose).

She told me all about the Lollicup coffeehouse, a fun cafe she'd discovered during her trip to Boulder. "They serve tapioca pearls in the coffee, Tess. It's different, weird—and marvelous." As though on cue, my coffee pot beeped. Naomi slipped out of bed. "I'll get it." She put on her robe and headed down the hall. When she returned, she set my mug down on my night stand. "What's with the clothes all over the living room?"

"Lana's clearing out her wardrobe, getting ready to move in with her fiancé Gable." Saying it aloud made it seem more real. Yes, from the looks of things, I'd be without a housemate soon. Did Naomi and I have a future together?

I sipped the savory Guatemalan Supreme and looked at my

new lover. Her attention was now on Wolf Blitzer. My eyes followed the curve of her cheek, the wave of her silvery mane, a profile both intelligent and, behind closed doors, soft and feminine. I was touched by an inexplicable tenderness.

In matters of the heart, it's wise to hold something back for a while, to restrain emotions when first getting to know someone. But there comes a point—an azimuth along the heart's horizon—where it's necessary to take the risk, to open your heart fully to the most loving and the most painful possibilities. I'd reached that azimuth.

"Naomi, when Lana moves out, I'll need to find another housemate. Or I could sell my house. I want you in my life, sweetheart. This—"us"—feels right to me. If you feel the same way, maybe we should try living together . . . " My inflection let it be a question.

She looked at me thoughtfully and sipped her coffee. When she spoke, she chose her words with care. "I don't know what the future holds, Tess, but I know I love you. I also really love my job, and I couldn't do what I'm doing from San Diego. Would you be willing to relocate? I want to move forward with whatever next steps seem right."

"I'll start checking real estate listings in L.A.," I answered with a grin.

Within seconds we had melted into a kiss that would lead to another kiss that would soon lead to much more. Or could have. This time it was my phone that disrupted the mood.

I was willing to ignore it, but Naomi pulled away. "Go ahead and answer; it might be important," she said as she tuned back into the political shenanigans on TV.

I picked up the call.

At first, the weakness in the voice made it difficult for me to identify the caller. "Beth, is that you? Are you all right?"

"I'm at the UNM hospital. In their Maternal Fetal Medicine Center."

Ever so softly I asked, "Did you lose the baby?"

"They tell me everything's all right." She sounded uncertain. "I had a partial placental abruption . . . " From the slur of her speech, I knew she was under the influence of sedatives or pain meds.

"Is it as serious as it sounds?"

"Very serious. The placenta became partially detached. If it had detached all the way, the baby would've died."

"But even tiny preemies can survive now, can't they?"

"My OB-GYN says there's little chance of survival until the fetus is at least twenty-five weeks old. I'm not quite there yet."

That was sobering. "What caused it? Were you in an accident? Did you fall?"

"No, the doctors say it's a problem with older mothers. But I think the stress of the arrest did it."

I thought so, too, but didn't say it. "How long will you be in the hospital?"

"Three more days. Then they'll let me go home for bed rest."

"Will your sister arrive in time to help take care of you? If not, I'll get on a plane and . . . "

"Katie's already here, Tess. You don't need to do anything. I just wanted you to know what happened and where I was, in case you wanted to me to reach me."

"Thanks for letting me know. You take good care of yourself and that little chitlin, OK?"

I remembered Armida telling me that the park ranger George Calvert and his wife had lost a baby. Sad—and bad—things do happen to good people. Which reminded me of the book by that name, which reminded me of Rabbi Harold Kushner who wrote it. Which of course reminded me of the lovely rabbi sitting in bed next to me.

I filled Naomi in on the situation.

"When I was married, I had two miscarriages," she said quietly. "It's tough to go through something like that."

"Would you pray for Beth's baby?"

"Of course," she answered. "And I'll add Beth's name to our list for healing prayers at the next service."

27

PRIVATE IDES

JULIUS CAESAR CAN HAVE the Ides of March. I say, beware the Ides of September.

September in San Diego usually brings cooler evenings, boisterous school yards, and a brush of gold to the sycamore leaves. But this September, emotional crises were in bloom.

It started one evening when Lana was soaking in a bubble bath. She'd put her engagement ring in the soap dish for safe keeping. (I know . . . but that's what she did.) Suddenly I heard splashes and thumps coming from the bathroom along with "Oops, no, drat, ouch!," the "Om mane padme om" of the clumsy. Loosely translated, it meant "the jewel is in the lotus drain because the soap dish spilled." Somehow when she pulled the rubber stopper to let the water out, her elbow knocked into the soap dish, sending her engagement ring into Drano land.

Tearful calls to Gable and an expensive plumbing job ensued. By the time the ring was rescued, palpable tension had arisen between Lana and Gable. As Lana put it, the incident was a "karmic trigger." Gable lectured her about irresponsibility, growing up, and doing something with her life. She gave the ring back, thinking he would calm down, make nice, and insist she accept it again. He didn't.

My own karmic trigger took the form of an interfaith Middle East peace conference scheduled to take place in Lebanon the week after Labor Day. Naomi would attend on behalf of her hope-in-the-genes organization. This conference represented a major career step for Naomi; power players from the Vatican, the World Council of Churches, the Progressive Muslim Union, and others would attend. She couldn't have been happier if they were transporting her there via a cloud of nitrous oxide.

Just before Labor Day, a series of car bombings began in Beirut. The next day Sasha Bakarandi, the CNN journalist, was taken hostage.

Snuggling in my arms the night before she left, Naomi assured me that the conference would take place in a safe part of the city. She wasn't in the least worried. But I was.

She emailed me the day she landed, joking about a lost suitcase, telling me the sky was cloudless and blue. That was our final communication: a friggin' baggage and weather report. From then on, my emails to her drifted silently into cyberspace without response. When I called her cell, I got voice mail. I left messages—more urgent with each passing day—but received no calls back.

When her voice mail was full, I phoned Kehillah Beth Am, the progressive Jewish congregation in L.A. that sponsored Naomi's organization. Again, I was directed to voice mail. Left messages. No call backs. I sent a certified letter to the congregation. I received a certified letter in return: "We assure you Rabbi Roth arrived safely at the peace conference. We regret that we can offer you no further assistance in your efforts to locate her. Should you find yourself in Los Angeles, please feel free to visit Kehillah Beth Am for worship and community."

In the mornings, I'd feel sure Naomi had been taken hostage by fanatics and that our government was censoring all communication about her situation. I'd cry and pray and eat chocolate. By afternoon, I'd feel equally certain she had run off with some gorgeous dyke she'd met at the Beirut airport. Nothing made sense. I felt like a hyena standing on the corner of Insanity and the Fourth Dimension.

I now knew what Lyle meant by "needed her too much." The heartache I woke up with every morning was a September 11 of romance; a hijacking of the heart. I got little sleep, and when I did, I dreamt nightmarish jumbles of Rashid at FBI headquarters telling Kendra's parents that she had been killed by a suicide bomber. Or Naomi on her way to the Middle East on a jet piloted by Jorge, with Lyle, head bandaged, in the passenger's seat next to her. I would have welcomed the ant preacher.

Near midnight on the Ides of September, Lana and I sat on opposite ends of the living room sofa in our pj's, the dogs nestled at our feet. We'd finished half a bottle of Chablis, but were both still reasonably sober. Heartbroken by circumstances and bored by Stephen Colbert, we indulged in an informal competition about whose emotional wounds were uglier.

I initiated. "Take a syphillis canker and pour used motor oil on it. That's how gross this heartache feels."

"OK . . . when salad goes bad and the lettuce turns to green slime—mix that with baby diaper poo. That's how this broken engagement feels." Lana let out a sour giggle.

Well, maybe we weren't completely sober.

I thought about the dear friend at the opposite end of the sofa. The blue eyes that had so charmed me years ago, with the hint of Laplander in their epicanthic fold. The healed nick in her upper lip. The voice like an opium den. The loopy mind and the generous soul. I was fortunate to have such a good friend to commiserate with. But all I wanted was to stop hurting; I wanted to get blitzed.

I went to the kitchen to see if a cold Corona might be hiding in a corner of the fridge. Nothing. "Do we have any pot in the house?" I yelled from the kitchen.

Lana shook her head. "No, Gable doesn't like it, so I haven't had any around in months."

I returned to the living room sofa. "Damn."

Lana got up, walked over to me and used her best massage technique to loosen the tension in my neck and upper shoulders. "When I was a teenager," she reminisced, "some of my friends talked about getting high on aspirin and Coke. We've got aspirin and Coke in the house. I wonder if it works?"

"Never tried it; it's probably an urban legend." I thought about how Coke caused reactions with so many things. Then, suddenly my brain's Annie Oakley axons fired right on target and hit a bull's-eye. "Criminitlies!" I stood up and paced the living room. "The night I was at the Lightning Field, we were all talking about camping experiences. Kendra said that when she was little, some kids at a camp told her if she put a bunch of potato eyes in a bottle of Coke, the next morning the potato eyes would turn into cat's eye marbles."

"That's dangerous. Potato eyes are poisonous."

"I just realized that." I tossed a couch pillow into the air. "What if that Coke bottle sat there in the sun for a day or so, soaking up the toxins? What if Kendra abandoned the bottle where another kid could pick it up? She wouldn't have understood the safety issues; she was only five or six at the time."

"And if a baby, well, a toddler maybe, came by and drank from that Coke bottle . . . "

"Ranger Calvert and his wife lost a young child. If they ever went camping along the Illinois River. . . ." I looked at the clock. It was too late to call Armida, but email would reach her first thing in the morning.

From: freepi4all@gmail.com
To: A.Franklin7thDist@da.state.nm.us
RE: Kendra's murder
Armida—How did Ranger Calvert's child die? Very important; need info soonest!
Tess

I adorned the email with the red Priority exclamation point that means "pay attention" and clicked the Send button.

It was the first night I slept soundly in weeks.

28

CAN OPENER

LANA AND I BOTH awakened with a lift of spirit seen mainly in breakfast cereal commercials, a mood rare for heartbroken middle-aged women. She knew I would follow up on our Coke bottle insight, and graciously took Raj and Pookie to Dog Beach so I could concentrate. After waffles, kiwi fruit, coffee, and a shower, I opened the sliding glass door between my bedroom and the back patio to let in both breeze and bird song, closing only the screen. I glanced at the Tinker Toy suspects laid across the Saltillo tiles of the floor. Maybe soon I'd be able to put them away.

I resembled an electronics geek as I booted my computer—PDA to my left, cell phone to my right—but I was actually more like an electric can-opener about to shear the rim off Pandora's tin box.

I checked my email. Nothing from Naomi—oh, that throb in the solar plexus!

The signal of incoming email PINGed.

From: A.Franklin7thDist@da.state.nm.us
To: freepi4all@gmail.com
RE: Kendra's murder
Tess, George Calvert's child died of crib death in infancy. I'm probably violating his privacy by telling you this, and I don't see how it could be related to Kendra's murder. But I trust you had your reasons for asking. The baby's death devastated George and his wife.
Regards,
Armida

Well, screw me blue and paint me pretty. The insight about Kendra leaving the Coke bottle full of poisonous toxins still felt too significant to abandon. I closed my eyes and visualized Kendra as a young girl, being told tall tales by older campers. I imagined a toddler walking nearby, reaching for a Coke bottle.

Suddenly I remembered—Ned had lost a child, too. When I'd asked him about children, Ned had been vague, saying he had "one that lived"—his daughter. Ned had attended the University of Illinois veterinary school. It was at least possible that his family had camped along the Illinois River near St. Louis, where Kendra's family camped. It was worth a shot.

I thought about asking Armida for help, but she seemed peeved at me over my inquiry about Ranger Calvert's baby. Better try a different tactic. I phoned my ex-hubby Roark, punching in the necessary security codes to access his Beltway office.

"Tess-baby! How's that romance with the rabbi going?" His rich baritone boomed.

"Roark, I need you to verify a piece of information for me and I don't want to hear a single word of condescending crap about protecting me from danger. A life depends on this. Right now. Now! Got it?"

Uncertain and abashed, Roark said soberly, "I may not be able to . . . "

"Look, I know one of the people at the Lightning Field was an FBI agent and you couldn't break his cover. I know all about Rashid. I'm not interested in causing him trouble." I paused to let Roark digest this. "I need you to access the coroner's records on the child of Ned Merkur. He was one of the guests at the Lightning Field. I need to know exactly how his child died. Now, if I matter to you at all, 'darlin'," I mocked his southern charm, "get this information for me, STAT!"

Roark STATTED me back within three minutes. Maybe I should ride bare back on my high horse more often. "Ned Merkur's son, Timothy A. Merkur, was poisoned during a camping accident and died July 22, 19__. He was two and a half years old."

I tried to think clearly about next steps, but it was difficult to process. Could the charmingly paranoid Ned really be Kendra's killer? His belongings had been searched: What had he used for a weapon? Was he some kind of psycho? I hated to accept that because I liked him. But then, maybe you didn't need to be psychotic to avenge the death of your child.

While I had as many questions as I had answers, I decided the first thing to do was to let Armida know right away. I also wanted to get word to Beth, to relieve her anxieties about her arrest as quickly as possible. Because my solution to the Lightning Field murder involved a dead child, I worded my communication carefully so as not to upset the mother-to-be.

I addressed an email to Armida and Beth: "I know who killed Kendra. I had a breakthrough last night when Lana and

I began talking about aspirin and Coke. Sounds strange, I know, but I'm sure I've nailed it. Call me, Armida, as soon as you get a free moment. And Beth—get ready to lose that ankle monitor!"

Adrenaline poured through me: at least one area of my life was about to gain some resolution. Naturally, that led me to think of the area that was still starkly painful—Naomi. I decided to copy her on the email and let her know her true love was a successful sleuth. Hurriedly, I clicked the drop-down menu in the cc box of the message, selected Naomi, set the message to Priority, and clicked Send.

Another email PINGed. It was from a potential employer, Kemosabe Software. I'd sent them my resume in response to a job posting on Monster.com. The pay was generous and the job sounded like a good fit for me. The email from their human resources department instructed me to fill out a lengthy, convoluted job application, possibly designed by the offspring of Rube Goldberg and J. Edgar Hoover. What a pain in the butt—it took me over an hour to complete it.

I then spent twenty minutes answering emails from friends concerned about my recent depression. I had just wrapped that up when Armida called me back. I explained my theory about the murder, including what Roark disclosed about Ned's child's death. Armida had been unaware of the camping/Coke bottle conversation, but quickly put two and two together. "This is the break we've been looking for, Tess. But why did you copy Ned on your message? Were you trying to intimidate him? I don't think that was smart."

"What are you talking about?"

"You copied Ned on the email to me and Beth."

"No, I didn't." I opened my email program and brought up the Sent copy of that message. Sure enough, there was Ned's name, plain as day, as the Copy addressee. "Damn!" Ned and I had swapped email addresses back when we were at the Lightning Field, as did most of us. It was more a social courtesy about the shared experience than a real expectation that we'd ever hear from one another, a ritual Rashid had carefully avoided. I stared at the "Copy to" line. "I screwed up, Armida. I meant to copy my girlfriend Naomi. I was in a hurry, and thought I'd selected her name, but I guess I'd selected Ned's. Oh, man, I really stepped in it, didn't I?"

"Well, I asked the Las Vegas police to detain Ned immediately for further questioning. They should be picking him up any minute."

"Is our theory enough to arrest him?"

"Not by itself, no. But two days ago the Mexican authorities released some information from the man you knew as Jorge. He offered a sworn statement that when Ned sent him out for the expensive Scotch, he also asked him to pick up six alkaline batteries. We couldn't do anything on the basis of that statement alone, since we didn't find any electrical weapon in Ned's possession. But now, with the information you've uncovered, I think we have enough to put the fear of Jesus into Ned during an interrogation."

"Ned had to have found the cattle prod in the tack shed and disposed of it later, somewhere at the Field." I heard a distant beep.

"Got another call coming in, Tess. Good work; talk to you later."

I put the computer in stand-by, stood up and stretched. I

picked up the Ned Tinker Toy character and connected it to the Kendra Tinker Toy hub. It fit.

I heard the sliding screen door scrape open. As I turned to see what was happening, a cloth soaked in the noxious perfume of chloroform covered my nose and mouth. Pandora's box was open.

29

DOWN THE HATCH

I WOKE UP SLOWLY, which was merciful. My head felt woozy. I had no idea how long I'd been unconscious. I was in the passenger seat of a car, my hands cuffed and hidden under a light blanket spread across my lap. Ned was in the driver's seat, navigating a four-lane highway through hills and high desert. I smelled New Car air deodorizer cloaking stale cigarettes. This wasn't Ned's maroon Xterra; this was a generic rental sedan. REM were losing their religion on the car stereo. I used the blanket to wipe a stream of sleep drool from my mouth. "You taking me to the Gila Guts Saloon for tamales again?"

Ned smiled but his tone was sadder than a rental car ashtray. "I'm afraid not, Tess; I'm afraid not."

We passed a California State Highway 138 sign. Putting that together with the topography, I guessed we were near Antelope Valley, maybe, off the section of I-5 north of Los Angeles known as the Grapevine.

What to do? I scanned the car for a gun, but saw no

weapons. As long as he drove reasonably, I didn't see any advantage in body-slamming Ned while he was behind the wheel; at seventy miles per hour an accident could mean broken bones and punctured organs for both of us. And I wasn't capable of anything that required dexterity while handcuffed. You can't trip a fellow while he's driving and somehow I didn't think offering him sexual favors would succeed, for either of us. I tried to conjure an alternative escape plan.

We passed a roadside stand selling peaches and figs. Ned asked, "You don't have children, do you?"

"Not my thing."

"You'll never understand." He turned down the stereo. "You know about my son?"

"Yes."

"He was the most beautiful child." He swallowed the catch in his voice.

"I believe you, Ned, and I'm so sorry you lost him. But Kendra was only a kid herself at the time. I'm sure she had no idea . . . "

In a kindly, tempered voice Ned continued. "We expect to lose our parents. We know we could lose a spouse. But we never expect to lose a child. It violates something very deep in us; it leaves a pain you don't talk about, even to those closest to you. It makes people uncomfortable; they don't know what to say." Ned switched on the left blinker and turned down a side road. "I tried to handle the hurt, the anger. I even went to therapy."

"Didn't work, did it?" A safe observation, if ever there was one.

"I was mad as hell and stayed that way for a long time. But

years went by; we had our daughter Rachel. Then the government started screwing with me about my veterinary license. The Feds became a good target to aim my anger at. And for years, it sort of worked. My marriage fell apart and my daughter can't be bothered with me now, but still . . . I made a life for myself. I created the museum; my sense of humor returned. I used my veterinary skills in volunteer work at an animal shelter. I dated occasionally. I drink too much sometimes but overall, I was making it work . . . "

This country road had been the zenith of zilch, but finally a farm appeared on the right. Now that we were off the main highway, Ned's speed was probably about fifty-five or sixty miles per hour. If I could open the car door, jump out, and roll myself off the road toward the farmhouse, I could get help. I nudged the door handle. Ned caught the action out of the corner of his eye.

"No good, Tess. I've got the child safety locks on." He laughed bitterly to himself. "Child safety; that's rich. Anyway, I thought my heart had finally healed. Then suddenly, there was Kendra, sitting on the porch of the Lightning Field cabin, talking about how she'd put those potato eyes in the Coke bottle like it was just some big joke."

"Ned, she probably had no idea that any harm came from it."

"I'm sure she didn't; more's the pity." He glanced at the car clock, then backed off the accelerator, slowing to about forty on this two-lane road. "Imagine how I felt, Tess. All these years, wondering who had left that bottle. Then actually being within a few feet of her . . . I was in shock."

"How does killing Kendra make a sad situation any better?"

"It's God's justice."

"Come on, Ned; you're no Bible thumper. How can you say that?"

"I didn't go to the Lightning Field to kill Kendra. But the Universe set it up perfectly; everything fell into place. When Kendra admitted the Coke bottle incident, I could feel the old anger start to burn. Then she told us how Lyle sleeps through anything. That's when some kind of payback first entered my mind. When I was wandering around outside the cabin, I found an electric cattle prod in the tack shed. Not the best weapon, but a weapon, nevertheless. And the lightning storm —Tess, if God hadn't wanted it, how could all those things happen just right?"

I could've used some theological insight right then, but my favorite rabbi wasn't available. Not wanting to offer clichéd theodicy, I kept quiet.

Ned continued his explanation. "Tess, I actually said a little prayer, like 'God, if I'm misreading you; if you don't want me to avenge my son's death, then put up a road block.' But one by one, things continued to fall in place. Jorge was willing to buy fresh batteries for the cattle prod. When the lightning storm came—you know they don't happen all that often—I realized God was giving me the green light. I put a soporific in a glass of Scotch I poured for Rashid while we watched the storm. I carry several drugs like that in my vet's bag. I knew he'd sleep through the rest of the night. I used chloroform to sedate Kendra, then picked her right up out of bed. Lyle never even twitched through the whole thing."

"The guy should've majored in sleep," I said.

"I carried her out to the Lightning Field and with my flashlight, found a place where there was already a scorch mark on the ground from a lightning strike. You know the rest."

"What did you do with the cattle prod?"

"I walked a few hundred feet away and pushed it down a prairie dog burrow. Those suckers are deep. I made sure it went far enough that a metal detector skimming the ground wouldn't pick it up."

Ned probably also convinced himself that God provided prairie dog burrows at the Lightning Field just so he could dispose of a murder weapon. "So the day I found Kendra's body, you did mouth-to-mouth resuscitation because you knew your DNA would be all over her. Slick, Ned, very slick."

Ned turned onto a dirt road. We were now in the foothills of the Tehachapi Mountains.

"Where are we headed?"

"There's this guy who likes to visit my Off the Map Museum; comes in a couple times a week. Likes to chat. He's a First Sergeant stationed at Nellis. Used to work near here at Edwards Air Force Base until he was transferred a month ago. He's a kindred spirit—sick of the way the federal government hides a lot of dirty deeds from the taxpayers who support it. He's been telling me about the underground bases and interconnecting tunnels that stretch between Edwards Air Force Base and what's known as Tejon or Tehachapi Ranch. What's funny is, he's a smart enough guy, but he doesn't 'get' that the focus of my museum is on government disposal of hazardous toxins, not aliens. He thinks the government is hiding alien corpses out here in the underground facilities. I told him if I could gain access to these tunnels, I'd bring back an alien for my museum. The good First Sergeant gave me his Air Force security code for one of the tunnel entrances."

Ned pulled the car onto a flat area near a hill and parked. In the distance on the next hill over, two cows grazed. "Tess, I appreciated the fair warning you gave me when you copied me on your email to the D.A.'s investigator."

It didn't seem in my best interest to correct his assessment of my motives.

"Because you gave me a fair warning, I'm not going to kill you. I'll give you some chance of surviving. Now, it wouldn't be too bright of me to give you a big chance but, well, you'll see."

He unlocked his own door, shut it and walked around to my door, which he then unlocked. He pulled me out.

I was so close to him I could smell his sweat, his fear. I noticed he wore two different color socks. He had the look of someone on the Titanic who was sure that if he just wished hard enough, more lifeboats would appear. This was a broken, deluded man. Despite what he'd done to Kendra, there was still a part of Ned I connected with, something I thought was decent. I looked him directly in his once-twinkling blue eyes. "Ned, if you turn yourself in, a lawyer could probably argue a good case for extreme emotional distress brought on by meeting Kendra at the Lightning Field. You could give her parents closure. You could prevent my pregnant friend Beth from being tried for a murder she didn't commit. And I'll testify how you could've hurt me, but instead you let me go. A judge and jury would take all that into consideration."

I probably shouldn't have mentioned the judge and jury.

With a rueful expression, he took me by the elbow and led me toward the rocky hillside surrounded by a high barbed wire fence.

"As long as you're revealing secrets, how did you get to my house so fast after I sent the email?"

"I took the first available flight from McCarren to San Diego. It only takes an hour, you know. Your address is in the phone book. With GPS in the rental car, it took fifteen minutes from Lindbergh Field to your house."

Damn that job application! That's what held me up at home so long.

A vulture swooped overhead.

I tried a different strategy. "Ned, Armida called me this morning when she got my email. She knows all about Kendra and the Coke bottle, the whole connection. If you harm me, you'll only be getting yourself into worse legal trouble."

He halted our progress around the hillside and looked at me. "You're bluffing. She never called you."

"She did, Ned. Honest. Check my cell phone if you don't believe me."

"Yeah, right. Like I'd let you keep your cell phone in your pocket. Your cell's in your house in San Diego." Ned steered me behind a clump of palo verde trees that shielded part of the hillside. "And even if you're not bluffing—if I am taken into custody, I'll be the only one who knows where you are. I can trade that information to cut a deal with the D.A."

Too many people watch *Law & Order* nowadays.

Ned ran his hand along a rock in the hillside until he felt something, then slid open a piece of perfectly camouflaged plastic. Beneath it was a security code keypad. He indicated an area to my left behind a small boulder. There, set into the ground like a sewer grate was a dimpled metal plate about three feet by three feet, with a seam in the middle.

"When I punch in the security code, this entry hatch can be opened. I'll take off the handcuffs so you can climb down the stairwell ladder. Go slowly; the ladder is steep. When you get to the bottom, there'll be an unlocked door in front of you. But I wouldn't go through it if I were you. It opens onto a network of underground tunnels, some of which in turn lead to a secure location they call a CoG—continuity of government site—where the president can be housed in the event of a national emergency. Because of the high level of security, these tunnels are equipped with motion detectors that discharge automatic weapons at anything unauthorized that moves through them. You've got no food, no water, no weapon, and no flashlight."

"Where does the 'giving me a fair chance' part come in?"

"At a bigger entrance nearby, the Air Force sends in a change of security troops every day at 7:00 a.m., 3:00 p.m., and 11:00 p.m., seven days a week. When they enter, they disarm the security system for about sixty seconds while they pass through. Your hatch is on the same security circuit as the entrance they use, so this will be unlocked then, too. If you can figure out when the guard changes and time it just right, you should be able to open the hatch manually and crawl out. We're only three miles from a paved road. You're in pretty good shape; you can walk it."

Immediately I looked for my watch to see how long before the guard change. And saw my naked wrist.

He saw my disappointment. "Sorry, Tess, but I can't make this too easy for you."

He entered the security code on the key pad. I noticed the key pad was silent; no tones accompanied the key punches.

As soon as he entered the final number, he slid the metal hatch in the ground open. He unlocked my handcuffs at the last possible moment and placed his hand firmly on my shoulder. I tackled him, hoping to throw him off balance, but he expected it and braced himself. He barely moved an inch. "Get down there, now! If I have to push you down, you might roll through the door at the bottom into the tunnel and be greeted by a spray of bullets. You wouldn't want that."

No, I wouldn't want that.

I stepped through the open hatch, gripping the cool metal bars of the ladder. The hatch closed over me. It was darkest place I've ever been.

30

BLONDED

I DESCENDED THE LADDER, tentatively reaching into the unknown with one foot, then the other, seeking the next step. Twelve rungs later, I arrived at solid floor.

I had all the view of a macadamia nut inside an 87-percent Dagoba chocolate bar: everything surrounding me was dark. By fumbling around, I established the size of my subterranean cell—a stairwell perhaps eight feet square. I could feel texture and grooves on the walls; probably concrete blocks. No cobwebs; didn't hear any mice. The area smelled clean and the temperature was pleasant, like they were keeping it just right in case the president really did have to make it part of the White House home-away-from-home.

I was stumped as to why there were no lights. Perhaps they were only activated when authorized visitors made an appearance.

The walls formed three sides of the area and as Ned had indicated, on the fourth wall was an unlocked door.

Just for the hell of it, in case Ned was bluffing, I opened the door to the long tunnel, removed one of my Nikes, and while remaining in the stairwell, tossed the shoe into the tunnel. Immediately I heard the brutish thrum of automatic weapon fire. Ned wasn't bluffing and I had lost one shoe. Rest in peace, Nike.

Maybe the gunfire would summon an MP curious about who or what had breached security in the tunnel. I waited. No one came. But it made sense that sooner or later, someone would show up. If the Air Force had to hide a president in these Continuity of Government digs, they wouldn't want the tunnels littered with smelly corpses, alien or otherwise. Surely someone conducted periodic inspections. If I held the unlocked door open and kept watch . . . Then again, their "shoot first, ask questions later" approach might not bode well. After a boring half hour or so, I let the door to the tunnel close again.

My mouth felt dry. The last thing I'd had to drink was my morning coffee. Humans can only last about three days without water. I hoped they conducted stinky corpse inspections at least every two and a half days.

I slumped down into a corner, psychologically and emotionally exhausted. The black velvet silence felt peaceful, like a Harry Potter invisibility cloak wrapped around me, assuring me I didn't have to do anything, feel anything, buy anything, answer anything or care about anything. Or anyone.

The sadness and confusion over Naomi had been squeezed out of my consciousness while I focused on solving the murder. But now it pushed back into the forefront. I could only suppress that pain for so long.

Would I ever know what happened to the woman who so stirred my senses and my heart? Was an explanation being broadcast on the cable news even as I sat here in coal mine darkness? My mind scripted welcome home scenes for her—scenes of celebration, of explanation, of passionate reconnection. I tried not to go to scenes of beheadings by extremists. Was she the one true love I'd been hoping for, for so many years? If she were dead, would I ever know happiness again? I had been changed by knowing her; of that much I was certain.

My thoughts churned for what seemed like hours, mostly in a downward spiral. I cried a long time, then welcomed a soulful emptiness. All was silent. I was done. Done.

Suddenly up along the blackness of one wall a stunning light beamed—a burning star in this den of dark. Had someone opened a different hatch or a hidden window?

I stood up and waved my arms. "Hello? Anybody? I'm down here!" I called.

No one answered.

I squinted at the light and gradually made out Naomi's face shimmering at me. She looked serene and ethereal. "Darling, come with me," she called. "Come with me; it's all right."

"Are you . . . are you dead?"

She ignored my question. "It's very peaceful here."

"Oh, God, Naomi, I've missed you!"

"I've missed you, too. We can be together now. Come with me."

I slunk back to the floor and imagined, vividly, the tranquility of death.

If you brush Death's cheek once—and survive—you feel like you've blown all the luck you'll ever have; you'll never play the slots again.

Brush Death's cheek twice and you believe you've been

spared for a mission. You'll hawk spiritual Girl Scout cookies until no one opens the door when you knock.

Brush Death's cheek three times, and you just may succeed in your seduction.

This was the third murder case I'd been involved with and I'd had two very close calls. Maybe this captivity—no food, no water, no light—was God's way of reuniting me with my beloved Naomi.

A clear familiar voice chastised, "That's Ned-thinking! Didn't I drag you to church every Sunday? It's arrogant to second-guess God's intentions; you know that." The voice came from my left within a new light that sizzled like a sparkler firecracker. When my eyes adjusted, I saw my Grandma Camillo's face. "Pay attention, *ragazza dolce*. You don't need any other human being—not even Naomi—as your reason for living. When my Ernesto passed, I wore my sorrow like skin for a year. There were days I couldn't remember my own name because I didn't care. But one day you hear crickets or taste a homegrown tomato and you realize you're smiling. Life is a gift from God; say *grazie* and live it!"

The voice faded and the sparkler fizzled, leaving only darkness. Grandma Camillo's been dead about ten years; I must be hallucinating. People who used isolation tanks for meditation sometimes hallucinated from sensory deprivation. With nothing to see, nothing to listen to, and little to feel except the hard floor under my butt, my mind must have eclipsed the usual constraints of consciousness. Whatever Grandma Camillo really was—whether some part of me that did want to live or a spiritual hologram from the other side—my survival instincts kicked in.

I figured my best bet was to climb the ladder and keep my hand in contact with the hatch lid, hoping to sense a vibration, feel some electrical pulse, when the security system disarmed.

I stood up slowly. My joints were stiff and my right leg had fallen asleep. I hobbled around in the stairwell until I had full circulation in my legs. I manually located the lower ladder rungs and got my bearings. I climbed up high enough so I could feel the hatch lid with only a little arm stretching. I waited and listened.

Damn, I was thirsty. I took slow, deep breaths and tried to remain focused and calm. I would not look back in the direction where I had seen Naomi's face. I knew I couldn't, if I wanted to survive.

I don't know how long I was there before I felt it—an hour? Two hours maybe? It began as a low hum that I could feel in the metal with my fingers, more than something I could hear with my ears. Soon I felt the vibration change and when I pushed on the hatch, it opened!

It was night outside but a half moon lent the landscape a milky glow that dazzled me, so accustomed was I to visual void. I pushed off hard against a ladder rung to launch myself through the hatch onto the ground, but my foot (in a sock, missing its shoe) slipped from the rung and I lost my balance.

I landed on the hard floor of the stairwell and rolled into the door. My momentum and weight pushed the door open. I lay flat on the floor in the tunnel as a staccato of bullets whizzed above my head. Fortunately, the bullets were aimed to kill—at head and heart levels, not at the feet.

I probably had bruised a few ribs in the fall and my butt hurt like hell. With every ounce of determination I could muster, and while shock-adrenaline and injury-endorphins still flowed, I rolled back into the stairwell, scrambled back up the ladder, and grasped the hatch while the security alarm was still off. I pushed my body up through the hatch once more, and this time landed safely on the ground.

I looked up and saw a security squad in camouflage uniforms with rifles pointed at me. I'm not sure what made me do it—perhaps those cold war movies where a captured spy must prove he or she is an American—but I started singing "Born in the USA."

My parched throat barely cooperated. The song came out more like an enthusiastic whisper, but it must've worked. Rifle barrels lowered.

A lanky young airman walked over and offered me a hand up. In a pronounced Georgia drawl he said, "Ah lahk Springstein, too, but ma fav'rite uh his songs is Blonded by the Laht."

31
FIRST DANCE

LATE OCTOBER . . .

I unfolded the printed email and read it for the 157th time.

From: N.Roth@Force4Peace.org
To: freepi4all@gmail.com
Dear Tess,
I realize no matter how I put this, it will hurt. But I have quite obviously failed to be a *mensch* and for that I owe you some explanation.

Within moments of landing at Beirut Rafic Hariri International, I met someone I bonded with instantly—Arnaud Robeyns. We sat next to one another on the ride to the peace conference; we shared meals; had drinks every night at the hotel. No, I haven't gone back to men; we're not involved that way. Arnaud is the director of Force for Peace in Brussels, an international interfaith collaborative working on many fronts—Darfur, Afghanistan, Palestine, etc. We experienced a special intellectual synergy and sparked mutual enthusiasm for present and future projects. In the middle of my second day at the conference, Arnaud offered me a job working with him in Brussels that started immediately. I accepted.

I know it was selfish. I know you and I had talked about a future together. But I couldn't see you packing up everything to move to Belgium, and I couldn't give up such a golden opportunity.

When I gave notice to Kehillah Beth Am, I told them you were stalking me and asked them not to give you information as to my whereabouts. I'm sorry, Tess. Your exuberant passion for me and for our relationship scared me. You liberated me sexually in ways I never dreamed of, and for that I'm more grateful than you know. I'd never been very good at any kind of intimacy, and you helped me change some of that. Still, I do better with ideas and organizations than with people's hearts, and I must use the talents I have for my calling.

No, I don't want to talk this over. I don't really want any further contact with you; it would benefit neither of us. I don't ask your forgiveness. I only ask that you remain open to the possibility that this worked out the way it was supposed to.

Shalom,
Naomi

I folded the email again, slipped it into my carry-on bag, and clicked off the overhead reading light.

In the seat next to me, Lana asked, "How many times have you read that, Tess?"

"One hundred and fifty-seven." I thought she'd be impressed that I actually knew. She wasn't.

"Why don't you let me keep it for you while we're in Albuquerque? After all, this trip is supposed to do us both some good, and reading that will only bring you down."

With a shrug, I retrieved the email from my carry-on and handed it to her. At least I'm still the keeper of the booties.

Two weeks ago Beth had delivered a beautiful baby girl, only a week early. The six-pound, eight-ounce baby was healthy, and Beth was recovering well. Lana and I decided to celebrate and to cheer our own spirits by flying to Albuquerque, to up the "Aunties" so to speak. At a baby clothes boutique, I'd found the perfect pair of booties. Knitted from a soft green wool blend, they had frolicking lamb appliqués on the cuffs and white lace ribbon to secure them around tiny ankles.

I know, I know. But babies—and especially baby booties—do this to us. Go bootie shopping yourself some time and see what happens. Naturally we'd picked up about fifteen additional gifts for the new arrival. It's hard for two childless women not to overdo in the baby gift department.

Contrary to all expectations of U.S. air transportation, we landed safely and on time, and took a taxi to Beth's house. She was putting up both of us, which would save us hotel money and give her four extra hands for diaper changes, laundry, and cooking.

Beth's sister Katie greeted us at the door, all Green Bay Packer tee shirt and broad smile. She walked us into the den where Beth was burping the little one. Katie nudged me with her elbow. "We've got a surprise for you!"

Lana and I kissed and hugged Beth, then I examined the minute bundle of stretch Onesie and pink skin. "So this is Ms. Bailey Butler."

Katie and Beth tittered at an inside joke. "No! That's our surprise." Beth draped a blanket over my shoulder and handed her new daughter to me. "Tess, meet Tessa Leigh Butler."

I was speechless. I sat down on the couch and studied the infant's long eyelashes, fuzzy strawberry blond hair, gray eyes, and satisfied expression. "I thought you decided on the name Bailey, whether it was a boy or a girl?"

"That was before you nearly died trying to get me out of the murder charge."

Lana told me later that I could've lit up half of Albuquerque the way I was glowing.

"And the middle name Leigh?"

Katie answered that one. "Our mom was crazy about the actress Vivian Leigh and we wanted to give her that tribute. Tessa Leigh sounded better than Tessa Vivian."

I gently rocked in my arms the tiny girl who I hoped had a great big life ahead of her. "Tessa Leigh, I'm Tessa Lynn. You can call me Tess. Everybody else does, except my grandmother when she's upset with me."

Beth transferred the baby from my arms to Lana's, knowing Lana would die if she didn't soon get to hold her.

Suddenly something struck me. "Lana, have you ever heard me use the word *ragazza*?"

"No. What is it? A kind of pasta?"

"I'm not sure," I replied honestly. "But when I had that vision in the underground stairwell, my grandmother used that word."

I'm not one to readily embrace woo woo explanations of things. It's possible I'd heard my grandmother use the word when I was young and had filed it in my memory bank. Nevertheless, the realization gave me an eerie rush.

Beth said, "Naming her for you just seemed the right thing to do, after all you went through to solve Kendra's murder."

"It must've been hell for you out there in those tunnels," Katie remarked.

I did a quick mental inventory of my personal idea of hell:

No Ron Jeremy, no singing munchkins, no hypodermic needles. "No, but it wasn't a day in Lahaina, either."

"Beth never filled me in on what happened after you were rescued. How did those Air Force guys know not to shoot you?" asked Beth's sister.

"Armida had requested the Las Vegas police pick up Ned for questioning. When they discovered he'd taken off somewhere, Armida figured I was in trouble. Through his credit cards, she traced his flight to San Diego and his rental car. The car had GPS, so Armida was able to track him to the Antelope Valley area. When he was taken into custody, Ned tried to trade my whereabouts for a deal. But Armida had sent bulletins to all law enforcement units in the Antelope Valley area, including those at Edwards Air Force Base. When their security forces noticed unauthorized movement in one of the tunnel branches, they were aware it might be me. Those airmen were on the way to try to find me, not shoot me."

Two evenings and many burps, blankets, booties, and diapers later, we headed to a community dance. Every summer Albuquerque's music community hosts a fabulous production called Salsa Under the Stars—a big anything-goes outdoor dance with mostly Latin music. It mirrors the expansive mood of summer as hundreds of folks sip margaritas and show off their dance steps under a canopy of stars.

Because of the event's popularity, this year they were adding a new dance to their program: the Fall Fandango. It would be cooler out, but the Chamber of Commerce and the New Mexico Jazz Workshop had supported the idea, along with several commercial sponsors. The Albuquerque Museum of Art and History agreed to host the event in their outdoor amphitheater.

We arrived fairly early, which was fortunate because the seats were filling up fast. The walkways around the amphitheater were dotted with candles in paper bags called luminaria, or *farolitas*. These and the lights above the bandstand provided just enough illumination for us to thread our way to our seats.

The modest bandstand was stacked with speakers and microphones, bongos, an electric keyboard, and guitar cases. Brightly colored banners against the back wall advertised the Jazz Workshop, commercial sponsors, and other community events.

Many of the Bryce crew attended the event and I had a chance to catch up on gossip, jokes, and programming war stories with Garrick, Jeannette, Dano, and others. Lana went to a vendor and brought back hot chocolate for Beth and hot toddies for us.

Bundled in sweaters, sweatshirts, long underwear, or long skirts, people slid into the bleachers around us. The evening was mild for October, so most of us didn't need coats. Teens sat next to seniors; Boomers and Gen Y's greeted one another. Every color and ethnic mix you could imagine was represented. Conversation buzzed in English, Spanish, even Navaho. Children and babies like Tessa Leigh were a welcome part of the gathering, as were folks in walkers and wheelchairs.

Latin music energizes; the first song lifted the crowd! Initially, only confident, experienced dancers hit the boards, but soon so many folks drifted to the dance floor that there was hardly room to move. Lana and I shook off the evening chill with a few casual numbers.

Beth didn't dance; she said her strength just wasn't up to it yet, but she enjoyed watching everyone else.

After a while, a new band took the spotlight, one with an irresistible spirit and sound. With a look, a non-verbal question, and a nod, I lifted Tessa Leigh, bundled against the evening air in blankets, from her mother's arms and brought her to the dance floor. Time for her first dance!

Holding her snugly, I tangoed with her, much as I had tangoed with my pillow that morning in June. A *giro* here; a *barrida* there! I swirled Tessa Leigh in my arms and caught the beaming face of a young woman with Down's Syndrome dancing near me: Sheer joy. I wondered if she'd been in Kendra's art workshop. An elegantly dressed senior couple were kindling their own subtle fires to the salsa rhythm: you could see it in the way they looked at each other, the solicitous yet sensuous way they touched. I turned again on the dance floor and spotted Janka, the Hungarian apartment manager. She was having the time of her life with a Tom Selleck look-alike. A little boy climbed onto the bandstand and tried the bongos for himself, much to the bemusement of the bongo player.

At the end of the song, I brought Tessa Leigh back to Beth and thanked her for allowing me the privilege of her first dance. I looked around me at every skin color, age, sexual orientation, and socioeconomic group; people who knew me well and people I'd never met; people who danced superbly (like Tessa Leigh!) and those whose talents obviously lay in other areas. I was stirred by luminaria, friendship, salsa, and sass; by notes of brass, strums of guitar, drumbeats, and vibrant vocals that merged into a powerful stream, cleansing some heaviness from me.

While I chatted with Beth and Katie, Lana's cell phone rang, and she retreated to the relative quiet of a corner near the rest rooms.

A few minutes later she returned to us with a landmark smile and tears in her eyes. "That was Gable!" she announced. "He misses me terribly and wants to give it another try!"

I was truly happy for her and gave her a hug big enough to keep a bear in the Yukon warm for a week.

Life is forever a first dance, a dance with a partner whose steps we cannot predict. The band began to play "Chicharronero," one of my favorites. I walked out onto the floor alone, immersed myself in the warm energy of moving bodies, and caught the beat.